Dear Mystery Lover,

Travel writer and amateur sleuth Emily Stone thought she knew all there was to know about Branson, Missouri. She'd been to the stage shows, interviewed the biggest Branson celebrities, and catalogued all of the city's voluminous attractions. She found herself so captivated by the bright lights and down-home charm that she decided to make Branson her permanent home. And romance soon followed in the form of Marty Rose.

But Marty's closest companions start turning up dead and Emily may be next on the list. Could her sweetheart be a killer? *Evil Harmony* uses this Hitchcockian element to great effect and reminded me of Mary Higgins Clark's work. And, you couldn't have a more exciting setting than the country music mecca.

Like her protagonist, Kathryn Buckstaff knows Branson like the back of her hand. She lives there and is the author of the popular travel guide *Branson and Beyond* and the first Emily Stone mystery, *No One Dies in Branson*.

Keep your eye out for *Dead Letter*—and build yourself a library of paperback mysteries to die for.

Yours in crime,

Shawn Coyne
Senior Editor
St. Martin's DEAD LETTER Paperback Mysteries

Other titles from St. Martin's Dead Letter Mysteries

FROM *EVIL HARMONY*:

Since Emily had been dating Marty, she'd met all the Branson entertainers and had learned that most were pretty ordinary people until they walked into the stage lights. A few seemed never to recognize her from one encounter to the next, lost in their own importance. But when Tony Orlando walked over to wish Marty a happy birthday, Emily knew she'd be included in the conversation. Tony was a real charmer, brimming with enthusiasm. Too bad he was happily married, Emily had mused after their first meeting. And when Boxcar Willie came over, Emily stood up, eager for the hearty hug he always gave her. Marty never showed a hint of jealousy on these occasions. Emily wondered if that was a good sign or not.

Also by Kathryn Buckstaff

NO ONE DIES IN BRANSON (mystery)
BRANSON AND BEYOND (nonfiction)

EVIL HARMONY

KATHRYN BUCKSTAFF

St. Martin's Paperbacks

This is a work of fiction. Any similarity to actual incidents and any resemblance to persons living or dead is purely coincidental.

EVIL HARMONY

Copyright © 1996 by Kathryn Buckstaff.

ISBN: 0-312-95930-3

Printed in the United States of America

St. Martin's Paperbacks edition/August 1996

10 9 8 7 6 5 4 3 2 1

This book is dedicated to
my best friend and collaborator,
Robert Palms.

We will not live in beautiful harmony
because there is no such thing in this world,
nor should there be. We promise only to do
our best and live out our lives. Dear God,
that's all we can promise in truth.

—Lillian Hellman, *Candide*

⋆ FIRST SOUNDS ⋆

It's silent on Music Row. From the heart of Nashville where more than a hundred recording studios churn out the latest country hits, most of the promoters and publishers have retreated to the suburbs this Friday night, glad for a weekend's break before they have to face another waiting room filled with desperate clients.

Downtown, Tootsie's Orchid Lounge is packed. A young man in tight jeans and a black cowboy hat sits at the bar and orders his third beer. Behind him on the small stage, another young man in a black cowboy hat and tight jeans plays the song he wrote last month. There's no backup band. Just his cheap guitar. No one in Tootsie's pays much attention. Some are tourists who are there to look at the yellowed photos covering every inch of the walls, eight-by-ten glossies of the legends who played the Ryman Auditorium across the alley from Tootsie's back door. The rest are other songwriters, waiting their turn at the microphone.

The singer finishes to a smattering of applause. He sits down at the bar. "Boilermaker," he says.

"That sounded good," the young man says. "My name's Johnny." He extends his hand.

"Mark," the other says. "Thanks."

"Been in Nashville long?" Johnny asks.

The bartender brings a beer and a shot, and Mark slips four ones out of his thin wallet.

"A couple months," Mark says. "You?"

"Six months."

"Any luck?" Mark asks before he downs the shooter.

"I've got a meeting with my agent Monday," Johnny says. "I think he's got me a deal."

They lapse into silence, knowing any more conversation would just be swapping lies.

Behind them, a middle-aged cowboy takes the stage and tunes up his guitar.

On the tenth floor of a high-rise office on Music Row, a heavyset man with the phone to his ear runs his hand over his moist forehead, slicking back thin strands of oily hair. He paces the dimly lit office past a black leather sofa and around a large rosewood desk strewn with papers.

"Just what is it exactly that you want me to do?"

He stops and looks out the large plate-glass window. Across Demonbreun Street he sees the neon flashers still throbbing outside the Barbara Mandrell Country Museum where visitors pay five bucks to see a mock-up of the singer's high school–era bedroom.

"I can't do that, you psycho. I wouldn't do it even if I could. Where are you calling from?"

He listens. "No, I sure don't want to meet with you to talk about this. This is all the talking I'm going to do. You're insane to think you could get me to go along with this. The answer is no. Absolutely no."

He slams down the phone and sits heavily in his leather desk chair as his trim secretary comes in.

"Who was that calling so late?" she asks.

"Who do you think? Another nutty songwriter," he snaps. "I'm getting out of this business as soon as I can and buying me a little villa in Mexico.''

She smiles because she's heard him say this every Friday night for the ten years she's been his secretary.

''Will you need me anymore tonight?''

''No, thanks, Judy. I'm going to have a drink and head for home.''

''All right,'' she says. ''I'll see you Monday.''

She picks up her purse from under her desk in the reception room and closes the outer office door, where a brass name plate reads THE ZIMREST AGENCY.

Zach Zimrest brushes a speck of lint off the sleeve of his dark blue suit jacket and goes to the mirror-topped bar in the corner. He picks out a heavy crystal highball glass and pours a generous amount of Johnnie Walker Black. He drops in two ice cubes from the ice machine under the bar. Zimrest leans back against the bar, downs the potion, then goes to his desk. From the top drawer, he takes out a .38 caliber snub-nosed pistol. He flips open the cylinder, and seeing that it's fully loaded, puts the pistol back in the drawer.

Downstairs, Judy walks out of the elevator and through the front doors toward the parking lot across the street. She doesn't notice a figure in the shadows beside a telephone booth.

Zimrest finishes his drink and goes back to the bar to mix another. He loosens his tie, and sighs through pursed lips. As he swirls the ice cubes, the glass shatters in his hand. Zimrest looks down, stunned by the red stain spreading across the front of his white shirt. Two more shots hit him square in the chest, and he drops to the plush carpeting like a sabered bull. In his last moment, his glazed eyes rest on a framed photograph on the wall. ''To my favorite agent. Best always. Marty Rose.''

★ CHAPTER 1 ★

Marty Rose glowed in the spotlight, the deep pink sequins of his form-fitting western suit glittering with every movement and sparkling on the adoring faces of the women who lined the front row of the packed theater.

"I won't ever love again if I lose you," Rose sang, the twelve-piece band rising to a crescendo behind him. Applause started before the last notes were out.

"Thank you, folks," Rose said when the ovation waned. "You're a great audience, and I wouldn't be up here without you."

Rose turned and picked up a guitar from a stand behind him.

"I'd like to do one now that I hope you'll remember. You made it a number-one hit for Marty Rose in 1987."

As the band played the opening notes, another wave of applause came from the three-thousand-seat auditorium, and Marty pointed at the audience, acknowledging their recognition.

In the wings, Emily Stone smiled. She thought she might be in love with Marty. When she'd first seen him perform, shortly after she moved to Branson a year ago, she'd been starstruck by his magnetism onstage. Her friend Lyle Malone, a longtime Branson performer, had introduced the two, and Marty had asked Emily to write some publicity releases for him. She'd been happy for the work.

Three years ago, she'd been a travel reporter for the *Tampa Tribune*. Although she'd been born in the Ozarks, Emily's assignment to do a travel story on the growing music mecca had been her first trip back since childhood when her mom and dad had moved the family to Florida. The year after that fateful assignment to Branson, her husband Jim had been killed, an innocent bystander in a convenience store robbery. Emily wanted out of the city, and had decided Branson would be a safer place to live. She was working hard to build a base for her freelance writing, and her association with a big star didn't hurt her credentials.

But it was more than his fame that drew Emily to Marty. In the six months they had been dating, laughter had become part of Emily's life again. The hard, lonely feeling that Jim's death had left in her heart was fading. Still, looking across the stage at Marty, Emily felt that she didn't really know the man; she suspected that living in the spotlight for so long had made him protective of his privacy. On the other hand, sometimes she wondered if his years as a star had convinced him he really was a cut above everyone else.

Beside her, Anna nudged Emily with her hip.

"He's getting a great reaction tonight," said Emily's sixty-two-year-old mother.

"He always gets a great reaction," Emily whispered back. "I'm going to get something to drink."

Emily and Anna carefully and quietly wove their way around crew members standing by backstage to adjust lights or change scenery. They stepped over bundles of cables snaking from instruments onstage to amplifiers and sound mixing boards.

"Be careful," Emily whispered over her shoulder.

"I'm always careful," Anna said.

Emily smiled in the darkness. When Emily had decided to move back to the Ozarks, she had agonized over whether or not to invite her mother to move with her. She knew it wouldn't be easy to live together. But her father had died years before, and Anna was alone. In the end, Emily decided that bringing Anna back to Branson was the right thing to do, and as she'd become closer to her mother, she found that living with her wasn't as tough as she had feared.

Emily pushed aside a black curtain and opened a door leading into a brightly lit hallway. They passed the Green Room and the second door marked with a large brass star. A sign beneath the star said PRIVATE.

They walked by one dressing room for male band members and another for Marty's three female backup singers. Emily glanced in and saw the rows of round lightbulbs encircling the mirrors, countertops lined with jars of makeup and powder, clothes strewn on the floor, and three empty wig stands.

"How's it going tonight, Earl?" Emily called to a grayhaired man sitting on a stool beside the door leading to the rear parking lot.

Earl had been Marty's security guard since Marty opened the Crystal Rose Theatre ten years ago. He was a retired sheriff's deputy from a little town in Oklahoma who had moved to Branson after he'd retired. But Earl had gotten bored with fishing and playing pinochle. So like many other retirees, Earl took advantage of the wealth of employment offered by the boom town.

"Just fine except for that long line of ladies outside waiting for Marty." Earl grinned.

Since Emily had become "my lady," as Marty referred to her, Earl had taken to teasing Emily about Marty's many fans, even though the majority of his fans were women nearer Anna's age than Emily's.

With a dismissing wave, Emily walked into an open room where there were remnants of food on a buffet table. Anna took a finger sandwich from a nearly empty tray while Emily went to a Styrofoam cooler where cans of pop floated in melting ice.

"I don't know why I'm so thirsty," Emily said after a drink of Diet 7-Up.

"Probably you're nervous because you know he's going to get you out on that stage tonight," Anna said, fishing for a can of Coke.

Anna turned sideways to a full-length mirror that hung on one wall.

"I hate all the mirrors back here," she said, smoothing her green silk dress over her ample hips. "I told you this dress was a little too tight. I should have bought the blue one. This green just isn't right on me," she said, poking at her gray curls. "It makes me look sickly."

"It's not too tight, and you don't look sickly. The blue one had those weird ruffles around the hips. You would have looked like an old hula dancer prancing out onstage. And this one saved you about fifty dollars, don't forget."

"I wouldn't have cared," Anna said. "I just want to look good for my debut."

"You'll be fine. All you have to do is walk out, take the check, say 'On behalf of the Women's Crisis Center, thank you very much,' and boogie offstage."

"I'm not boogying anywhere," Anna said, picking a morsel of sandwich from between her front teeth. "And anyway, I won't be going out there alone. I know he'll get you out there, too."

"He will not. I told him not to. All I did was the publicity. You organized the whole bash."

"Since when did Mr. Rose start doing what you tell him?" Anna teased.

"I just *suggested* to him that I really didn't want to be called out there with you." Emily approached the mirror and turned sideways as Anna had done.

"I look like a backup singer. *'Only you,'* " she crooned into her pop can.

"You look beautiful," Anna said, admiring the sheath sequined in tones from pale pink to deep rose. It fit Emily's figure, still svelte at forty, like a glove and set off her thick, shoulder-length dark hair.

"And it was free, I might point out. That Marty Rose sure knows how to dress his girls," Anna taunted in a deep southern accent.

"I kind of liked it," Emily said. "When that woman from the dress shop called to ask when she could come by with a selection for me to look at, I thought it was a prank call. It's just one of those 'southern gentlemen' things. I asked Marty why he did it, and he said, 'Because I can.' So why should I be offended?"

"You shouldn't be offended," Anna said, swallowing the last of another little sandwich. "I wish Tommy would buy me a new wardrobe."

"So do I," Emily said. "Maybe then you'd clean some of that trash out of your closets."

Tommy Jamison was Marty's business partner and had bought and sold several businesses during the five years he'd been in Branson. Emily thought he looked just like the weasel she suspected that he was. He was a long, thin man with a skinny face topped with wiry salt-and-pepper hair. She had taken an immediate dislike to him, but she didn't share that opinion with Anna. Anna had met Tommy at Marty's theater one day while Emily was working for him. Tommy had invited Anna to dinner the first night, and had been out with her nearly every week since.

"With all his money, he could probably have any young woman he wants," Anna had said proudly. "But he wants me. He has good taste."

Emily privately figured Tommy had a few younger

women on the side, but Anna was happy, so Emily kept quiet.

"I just like his jokes," Anna had told Emily after their first date. "He makes me laugh, and that's more than you can say for most of these boring old geezers."

"Are you ready? We'd better get back out there," Emily said.

Onstage, Marty was into a joking routine with his steel guitar player, and the audience was howling. It was the same routine every night, written and memorized but designed to look spontaneous.

"People want to think they're seeing something off-the-cuff," Marty had explained. "They like to think something happened onstage when they were here that nobody else has ever seen, so let 'em. Show biz is all about illusions."

As the laughter faded, Marty went into the song Emily knew would be the last of the show.

"Get ready, Loretta," whispered Emily. Anna had every album Loretta Lynn had ever recorded.

"Hush," Anna hissed, nervously smoothing her dress.

In the auditorium, the audience swayed and clapped. Emily could see the first few rows, and everyone had a smile on their faces. Before the last chord ended, the audience rose for a standing ovation. Marty stood, nodding, bowing, waving for two minutes. Normally, he would have left the stage and entered the wings to dab at the sweat on his face before going out to do an encore. The encore was always "They Call the Wind Mariah." That was designed to go with one of the more innovative features of Marty's theater, his rain curtain. From horizontal piping mounted above the proscenium, beads of water fell forty feet to a trough just behind the footlights, where it was recirculated. It always brought a gasp from the audience when the rain fell. Tonight, however, the audience would be cheated of that.

Marty held up his hands and the audience sat down.

"Thank you so very much, ladies and gentlemen," Marty said in his humble stage persona. "You've been a wonderful audience. As you know, we're all here for a very special reason tonight. When the Women's Crisis Center opened in this town two years ago, a lot of people said we didn't need a facility like that here in Branson, where we take care of our own. We'd all like to believe that's right, but even in the shelter of our Ozark hills, there are those whose troubles can't be solved with a hug and a hot meal."

"He's going to call you out," Anna whispered.

"No, he's not."

"Over the past two years, more than fifty women and their little ones have come to the shelter. It's a need we wish we didn't have, but as you've shown tonight, this community will rally whenever someone asks. And here's the woman who first started asking for this benefit concert tonight, the woman who put this whole show together and sold tickets on every corner. Help me welcome Anna Stone."

Emily watched her mother bustle out across the stage to where Marty stood waiting, holding a large cardboard replica of a check.

Emily was holding her breath, hoping her mother hadn't secretly prepared a little speech, hoping even more that she wouldn't come up with one right now.

"And I'd be remiss if I didn't recognize one other person tonight. . . ."

Geez, Emily thought, rolling her eyes and taking a deep breath.

"The genius behind the publicity campaign that got you all in here tonight, Anna's daughter, and the love of my life, Emily Stone."

Marty held out his hand toward the wings, grinning

proudly at Emily as though this were a script they had written together.

She hadn't wanted Marty to do this, but she had known all the same that she'd love the moment. She could feel the spotlights' heat, lighting up her dress as though she were plugged in. The applause from three thousand people felt good. In that instant, she had a taste of what Marty felt at every performance, the adulation that transformed a tired, temperamental singer backstage into a master showman in front of the spotlights. She walked into Marty's outstretched arm and thought it was a pretty nice place to be.

"Ladies," Marty said to Emily and Anna as the crowd grew quiet, "I'd like to present a check for the Women's Crisis Center, on behalf of all these good people here tonight, for sixty-five thousand dollars. I know you'll put it to good use."

Again, the audience rose to its feet, applauding. Anna reached for Marty's wireless microphone. Emily held her breath.

"Thank you so much," Anna said, speaking in a rather breathless voice that sounded vaguely like Carol Channing. "With your help, women in desperate situations, and their sweet, innocent children, will have the resources they need to make a fresh start."

That's enough, Mother, Emily thought. Marty saved the day.

"Give yourselves a round of applause," he told the audience, gently wresting the microphone from Anna's hand.

The applause continued as the three of them stepped back and the rose-colored velvet curtain descended.

Immediately there was a flurry of activity behind the curtain, band members stretching, packing away instruments, chatting about the show.

"You look beautiful, sweetness," Marty said quietly

to Emily. "Anna, you did that just fine, and you look like a million bucks."

Before Emily could say a word, Marty turned and joined the throngs headed toward the dressing rooms. Emily felt a familiar deflation at his sudden shift of attention. One moment they'd be having what Emily thought was a meaningful interlude, and the next moment Marty would be off into another line of thought, making her feel somehow inadequate. She knew he didn't mean anything by it; he wasn't even conscious of his abruptness. It was the nature of a star, she had decided, who for most of his life had tried to please everyone around him, but never really had time for anyone in depth. She was sure it was the prime reason that Marty had never been married. His bride was the stage, and every night was another honeymoon.

"How'd I do?" Anna asked with a proud smile.

"Was that supposed to be Carol Channing?" Emily asked as they headed backstage.

"I just wanted to be properly elegant," Anna said in the throaty accent. "I may talk like this all the time."

"Carol Channing plays the Ozarks," Emily said over her shoulder. "You better have a talk with your hairdresser."

The hallways backstage were a hive of activity. At the rear stage door, Earl stood with his arms crossed, speaking discouraging words to several gray-haired women who stood outside. A couple dozen people from the audience were being shepherded by ushers toward the Green Room. Two of Marty's backup singers, dressed in tight, glittering gowns, were blocking the hall talking to three good-looking men who appeared to have crashed the scene.

"I'm going to find Tommy," Anna said, scanning the crowd.

"Tell him diamonds are a girl's best friend," Emily

said as she squeezed through a group outside Marty's dressing room and knocked.

A young woman with curly, jet black hair opened the door a crack.

"It's me, Tammy," Emily said and went in.

Inside, Marty sat in front of his marble-topped dressing table, drinking water from a large mug.

"Hey, babe," he said when Emily came in. "What'd you think of the show?"

"It was great." Every show he did was the same as far as Emily could tell, but Marty always asked the people around him how it had been. She wondered what would happen if anyone offered criticism, but no one ever did. The only changes that were made in musical arrangements, the selection of songs, or the routines that band members and backup singers did with Marty came from Marty himself. He was the star, the theater owner, and the undisputed boss.

Marty took the white towel Tammy handed him. He loosened his string tie, unbuttoned the top of his white tuxedo shirt, and wiped the sweat from his face and neck. His beaded jacket hung over the back of a nearby chair.

"I got anyone waiting tonight?"

"A few," Tammy said. "One's a World War I vet in a wheelchair. He looks as old as God."

"Good." Marty grinned. "I love to talk to people my own age."

Emily perched on the edge of a maroon leather love seat on the opposite wall of the dressing room and watched Marty in the mirrors. He's the best-looking boyfriend I've ever had, she thought, as pleased as the head cheerleader who lands the star quarterback. He had black hair that was as shiny as crow feathers. Emily suspected he colored it to hide emerging gray, as she did, but she'd never asked him about it. His square jaw was clean shaven. His cheeks showed a few pockmarks from teenage acne, but it gave his face more character. He had full lips and just a hint of a cleft in his chin.

Tammy carried the beaded jacket to a long closet while another young woman helped Marty remove his black leather boots that, like everything else in the theater, carried the imprint of the rose that had become his symbol.

The woman set the boots at the end of a row of fifteen pairs of boots in a rainbow of colors. Marty slipped on sneakers and took off the damp shirt.

"Tammy, put in the tape that boy brought by this afternoon. He said he sings like Hank Williams," Marty said.

Emily watched him towel his tanned, well-muscled chest and felt a stir of excitement. She hadn't slept with Marty yet, even though he was clearly in favor of the idea. Emily wasn't sure she was ready to be intimate again with anyone, nor was she confident of the wisdom of becoming intimate with a star like Marty Rose. But the idea aroused her too. And she thought tonight might be the night. It was the start of a two-week summer break Marty and other performers took each year during the peak of summer when tourists were more interested in boating and swimming than sitting in theaters. It was the night of the summer solstice. And it was Marty's forty-sixth birthday.

After his post-show duties were finished, more than two hundred people would gather at Marty's elegant lakeside home, and Emily knew it would be an all-night affair. Since she'd been seeing Marty, she'd changed her daily schedule to match his, sleeping until close to noon each day so she'd have the energy to stay up with him until the wee hours when his night ended.

Marty donned a chambray shirt and a tan suede jacket with fringe. He smoothed back his sleek hair with his fingertips and put on a dark blue ball cap with the Dallas

Cowboys insignia. He went to the tape deck and shut off the whiny singer.

"That boy never listened to Hank," he said. He leaned down and gave Emily a quick kiss on the cheek. "I'll be out in a flash, and then it's party time." He was gone before she had time to speak.

Inside the Green Room, seven people smiled and stood up when Marty walked in.

"Hi, folks. Good to see you," he said, shaking hands with each in turn. Some just wanted a photo autographed and left with a smile. Two wanted to tell Marty about the times they'd seen him years ago at a state fair in Austin, or maybe it was a concert in Atlantic City. When he got to a wizened man in a wheelchair pushed by a young man who introduced him as his grandfather, Marty pulled up a chair and sat down in front of the veteran.

"I'm so glad to see you," Marty said. "Thank you for coming to hear me."

The old man had a story to tell about the war. He spoke with difficulty, and for three minutes Marty nodded and smiled. When the man stopped for a breath, apparently ready to continue the saga, Marty stood and reached for the man's hand.

"Thank you so much for coming tonight," he told him with sincerity in his voice. "Marty Rose appreciates your sacrifices."

To the man's grandson, he said, "You-all have a safe drive, and come back to see us real soon," and he was out the door.

Early in their relationship, Emily had quizzed Marty about how he felt toward his fans and their constant interruptions he encountered everywhere he went.

"Emily, I love these people. They made me what I am. Without them I'd be like a mongrel dog in a barren wilderness."

Emily often found it difficult to judge the depth of his

sentiment, but as she had gotten to know him better, she realized that in hundreds of interviews throughout his career, Marty had answered the same questions so many times that even the most sincere reply could sound rehearsed.

After Marty had left to greet his visitors in the Green Room, Emily sat at his dressing table, wiped off the remnants of her lipstick, and applied a fresh coat.

"John?" Tammy called into a two-way radio and got a crackling reply.

"Pull the limo up. He's in the Green Room."

"Have you got a date for tonight?" Emily asked Tammy.

"Are you kidding?" Tammy plopped herself on the love seat. "When do I have time to meet anyone? I spend all my time taking care of your boyfriend."

As usual, Tammy managed to turn aside Emily's attempts at friendship. She'd been Marty's secretary and right-hand woman for twelve years, and she was completely dedicated to him. He'd hired her when she was nineteen, just out of high school. She'd been a clerk in the pro shop at Marty's favorite golf course, when he was still playing the concert circuit.

"I could see loyalty in her eyes," said Marty, who considered himself a great judge of character.

Now at thirty-one, Tammy was beginning to think she'd missed something through her loyalty to Marty's demands. Emily was certain Tammy had begun her career with Marty believing the star would fall in love with her and elevate her from secretary to wife. But Tammy had learned over the years that Marty saw her as his steady little workhorse. It seemed clear to Emily that her own status as Marty's steady girl rankled Tammy and led to the complaining she did in front of Emily.

"Haven't you met anyone at that line dance class?"

"I quit it," Tammy said. Emily wished she could tell

Tammy that the deep crimson lipstick she always wore was unflattering to her sallow complexion. Tammy needed a vacation in Hawaii for two weeks. And losing fifteen pounds wouldn't hurt.

"Why'd you quit?" Emily asked. "I thought you were dying to learn to do the Chug-a-Lug."

"The teacher was too impatient, and the guys were poor little hillbillies without a dime. They all had skinny legs and beer bellies. They looked like dancing frogs," Tammy said, fluffing her hair. "Not my type. Let's go find Marty and get to the party. Maybe there will be some guys there under forty."

As the white limo pulled up to the back of the theater, guests still lingered in the theater's lobby. It was the size of a football field, and people strolled across the rose-colored carpeting past photographs of Marty and Chet Atkins, Marty and Bob Hope, Marty and Conway Twitty, and dozens of other stars. Scattered among the photographs were more than two dozen framed gold records. There were still people in the gift shop, too, looking at every conceivable merchandise bearing a rose design: coffee mugs, hat pins, note cards, even a display of rose-colored sunglasses.

Outside in the rose garden that Marty had added two years ago, spotlights shimmered on the twenty-foot sculpture of a rose. It was pieced together seamlessly from huge chunks of crystal. The top piece that formed the rosebud was sculpted from rose quartz. No one who came to the theater failed to take a picture of the work of art.

From the Faded Rose Saloon came the sounds of clinking glasses as a young couple celebrated the last day of their honeymoon.

"That's how I feel about you," the young man told his bride. "If you ever left me, I swear I couldn't ever love anyone else again."

"I'll never leave you," the young woman said, and kissed her husband.

In his office one floor above the dressing rooms, Marty sat with the phone to his ear, cradling his forehead in his hand. He looked twenty years older than he had an hour before in the shine of the spotlights.

"He fell off the roof? His house is only one story. How do you die falling off the roof? Where was Nita? Oh, God, how awful. She must be in shock. Where are the kids? Well, of course you should have called me. He was my best friend."

Marty leaned back in the big leather desk chair. He flung his ball cap onto the floor and ran his fingers through his hair.

"What time Tuesday? All right. Well, you call me when they finish the arrangements. Of course I'll be there. Yes. Yes, Mom. Well, you had to tell me. Birthdays aren't much anymore anyway. Yes, I will. I love you, too."

Marty hung up the phone. Tears welled in his eyes.

He and Chick Martin had been the same age, inseparable companions playing stickball in the dusty street where they had grown up in Wimberley, Texas. Marty closed his eyes. He could see the lanky twelve-year-old handing him the beat-up guitar as though it were yesterday.

"Just try it," Chick said. "It'll make your fingers hurt like a bitch at first, but look at the calluses you'll get." He showed Marty his thickened fingertips.

"Why do I have to learn guitar?" Marty whined. "Can't I just be the lead singer? You already play good."

"No, I'm the drummer now. How dumb are you? I can't play guitar while I'm drumming."

Chick sat on a wooden stool behind a ratty drum set. Marty had been listening to Chick's drumming for the past two months since Chick had saved thirty-five dollars from mowing yards and bought the dilapidated set from Jones' Pawnshop.

Every day after school, Chick put on the radio and tuned in the big country station in Austin and caught the beat of every song they played. It was 1961. Johnny Horton's "North to Alaska" and Roy Orbison's "Only the Lonely" repeated every couple of hours on the airwaves. Loretta Lynn joined the Grand Ol' Opry, Patsy Cline was singing "I Fall to Pieces," and Faron Young had a hit with "Hello Walls," a tune written by an unknown songwriter named Willie Nelson. But for Chick and Marty, Marty Robbins was the idol. They knew every inflection of "El Paso."

"Hey, what's the matter with you anyway, Marty?" Chick said, putting down his drumsticks and looking at Marty's long face. "Elvis is out of the army now, and he's gone off to Hollywood. So that leaves it open for us. If you play that guitar, we can be as big as any of these guys, and you'll be buying your mother a pink Cadillac."

"Shut up, Chicken. Just drum," said Marty, picking up the old guitar off the floor. He ran his fingers deftly over the frets. The boys were good, and they knew it.

⋆ CHAPTER 2 ⋆

As the limousine rounded the bend into Long Creek Cove, Emily could see the lights of Marty's home across the lake. The twinkling reflections on the water looked like a convention of fireflies dancing for the solstice. The mansion he called "the ranch" was built of native limestone and red cedar. In the daytime, either from the lake or the road above the cove, the place was barely visible, blending into the surrounding woods. But tonight, Jurassic Park–type torches flamed on either side of the huge wrought-iron gates, lighting the overhead "Rancho Rosa" sign. All the pathways leading down to the boat dock were lit, and Christmas lights blinked in the trees.

By the time Marty and Emily arrived it was nearly midnight, and most of the guests were already there. At the open front doors, which had been hand-carved from oak by a local craftsman, a young man in a tuxedo shirt and dark slacks greeted them.

"Happy birthday, Mr. Rose," he said.

"Thank you, son."

Marty had been quiet all the way from the theater. Maybe just birthday blues, Emily thought.

The polished limestone of the foyer glistened in the light from the huge chandelier overhead. As soon as they

entered, people surrounded Marty, congratulating him on
the show and wishing him a happy birthday. A table in
the foyer held a pile of gaily wrapped gifts, specifically
prohibited on the engraved invitations.

"Let me get my lady settled, and then maybe we'll do
a little picking," Marty said. He spoke to a waiter, then
came back to Emily who had been edging toward the
kitchen.

Holding her by the elbow, Marty guided her through
the vast living room where Mickey Gilley sat at the white
grand piano playing a soft honky-tonk tune.

"Bring your gee-tar, Hoss?" he called to Marty, who
waved in reply.

Through the picture windows that lined the length of
the rear of the house, Emily could see a crowd of people
gathered on the flagstone terrace surrounding the swimming pool. Beyond and down another level, more guests
sat on the large dock where Marty kept his sixty-five-foot
houseboat. Emily was looking forward to spending some
time on that boat this summer, hopefully alone with
Marty.

The air smelled of honeysuckle. From a reflecting pool
just outside the living room, a stream trickled over rocks
and down several waterfalls until it reached the lake.

"I've seen the house, and I'm in love," Emily had
told her mother after her first visit to the estate.

"Is there a mother-in-law apartment?" Anna had
asked.

"No, but there's a real nice storm shelter with a lock
on the outside," Emily told her.

Marty led Emily to a table near the pool where a young
couple sat. There were only two chairs at the table. They
rose to greet Marty and shake his hand, with the starstruck smiles Emily had seen so often.

"We loved the show tonight," the woman gushed.

"You seem to get better every year. What's your secret?"

As she talked, Marty pulled out one of the chairs in which they'd been sitting, indicating that Emily should be seated. Marty sat in the other chair. After a couple minutes of chatter, the couple drifted off, apparently oblivious to Marty's slick maneuver.

"Alone at last," Marty said. He stroked her cheek with one finger. "You are the most beautiful thing I've ever seen in my life. Tonight's our night, darlin'."

"You seem a little distant," Emily said. "Is everything okay?"

"Everything's never okay. There's sorrow all around us, and all we can do is keep singing."

She hated it when he gave her those kinds of answers. But it was his birthday, and she sure wasn't going to throw a fit over anything tonight. Maybe one day soon, but not tonight. So he didn't like to confide. There are a lot worse faults a man could have, she thought.

The waiter came and brought a whiskey and soda for Marty and for Emily a bottle of Dos Equis with a frosted mug sided by a slice of lime. Marty knew it was her drink of choice.

"Could I bring you an assortment from the buffet?" the waiter asked, indicating a long table on the far side of the pool where champagne fountains gurgled at either end. For those with beer tastes, a cooling table held iced long-neck bottles of whatever brand a cowboy could want. There were trays of boiled shrimp and silver dishes of cavier, platters of steaming crawdads, and a chef in a tall white hat carving prime rib. Emily vowed she would try to steer clear of the dessert table. She knew Tammy had ordered a guitar-shaped birthday cake, but she also knew there would be small pecan tortes, napoleons oozing cream filling, and little cheesecakes that she would have died for about midnight last night. Emily felt the pinch of her tight sequined dress, and reminded herself that the woman who accompanied Marty Rose had better keep her figure.

"There you are," squawked Anna. She was closely followed by Tommy Jamison. "I've been looking all over for you two. Did you just get here? I thought maybe you'd just forgotten about the party and snuck off to that master suite."

"Mother!" Emily admonished.

"Hello, Marty," Tommy said. "Nice show. Too bad about losing the sixty-five grand."

"It's called 'charity,' Tommy. Ever heard that word? I see you've found the bar," Marty said. "Why don't you get your lady a chair?"

"I got it," Anna called as she dragged a redwood chair away from a nearby table and placed it beside Emily's. Tommy pulled up a chair as well.

"Better watch yourself, boy," said Tommy pointing to Marty's nearly empty glass. "Wouldn't do for you to have a binge right now with Nashville two days away. You ready for Tuesday?"

"I'm not talking business tonight. It's my birthday, it's summer, and I'm on vacation," said Marty, signaling the waiter for another round. "You take care of yourself. Anna, you look like an emerald tonight, and you did a great job onstage. That last standing ovation was yours, you know."

Emily knew that her mother didn't ever blush, but you'd have thought she could the way she giggled and fanned her face when Marty paid her lavish compliments. Emily thought it was a little undignified.

From the bandstand where a six-man group had been playing Bob Wills songs, the band leader announced that Mr. Rose, the honored guest and "our generous benefactor," had arrived, and that it was time to wish him a happy birthday. A spotlight found the foursome, the band played, and the sound of two hundred people singing "Happy birthday, dear Marty" wafted out over Table Rock Lake.

"Maybe we can get the old man up here in a little while," the bandleader joked.

The waiter came back with a tray holding fresh drinks and platefuls of samples of everything on the buffet tables, including, Emily saw to her pleasure, tiny cheesecakes topped with gooey chocolate frosting.

For an hour, Emily sat listening to the patter between Marty and the many people who stopped by the table to visit. Anna and Tommy had gone off to dance. Tommy's dancing was one of his best qualities, Anna said.

"He's not afraid to look like a fool," she'd told Emily.

Since Emily had been dating Marty, she'd met all the Branson entertainers and had learned that most were pretty ordinary people until they walked into the stage lights. A few seemed never to recognize her from one encounter to the next, lost in their own importance. But when Tony Orlando walked over to wish Marty a happy birthday, Emily knew she'd be included in the conversation. Tony was a real charmer, brimming with enthusiasm. Too bad he was happily married, Emily had mused after their first meeting. And when Boxcar Willie came over, Emily stood up, eager for the hearty hug he always gave her. Marty never showed a hint of jealousy on these occasions. Emily wondered if that was a good sign or not.

After a while, Tammy came by to see if there was anything Marty needed.

"You just go have a good time," he told her. "Get you one of these ol' boys, and show me what you've been learning at that dance class."

Tammy rolled her eyes at Emily.

"Fat chance. There's not a single man here under fifty."

Finally, when Marty could no longer ignore the insistent calls that he take the bandstand, he gave Emily a warm kiss on the lips.

"You wait for me," he whispered. "I promise. Eventually they'll all go home."

Marty headed for the stage, and Emily got up to go to the bathroom. Since she considered herself privileged, she would use the lavish facility off the master bedroom. That bathroom was nearly as big as the living room of her house. There was a separate room for the commode, and Emily had smiled when she saw the telephone in there. There was a whirlpool tub that must take an hour to fill, and a shower with eight showerheads.

"You can have warm water on your feet, hot water on your neck, and cold water where a man needs it," Marty had told her during the tour he'd given her.

Actually, a shower would feel great right now, Emily thought, trying to wiggle her toes inside the snug high heels dyed to match the rose dress.

As she walked across the living room, Emily expected to hear the familiar strains of one of Marty's hits.

"Hello, my friends," he said. "I'm so happy you're all here to help me celebrate what will undoubtedly be the best season we've ever had in Branson." Applause. "But my heart is heavy tonight because I've received some bad news."

Emily stopped and went back to the doorway.

"My dear mother in Texas called me tonight to tell me of the untimely death of my lifelong friend Chick Martin. Chick gave me my first guitar, and friends, believe me, without him I wouldn't be standing here tonight."

His voice broke, and he paused.

"Chick could have been anything he wanted to be," he went on softly. "He was a great musician, a creative genius, but he decided his little boys and his wife were the most important thing in the world to him, and he stayed with them. I'm going to try to get through this song. I haven't sung it for a long time, but I want to do it for Chick. We wrote it together when we were just kids.'' Marty turned to the bandleader. ''Think you can remember a little of 'Two Hearts Tied'?'' he asked softly.

Emily could feel the lump in her throat and tears just behind her eyes. She'd never heard Marty talk about his childhood. She knew ''Two Hearts Tied'' had been a big hit, but she'd never heard him perform it.

Emily couldn't move as the sweet, sad strains of the old love song floated across the night.

''The angels fly with two hearts tied. . . .''

The fiddle took up the plaintive refrain, and Marty's voice broke more than once. People sitting by the pool and on the dock were motionless and silent. No one applauded when the music faded away.

''Thank you for that moment, my friends. Chick would have appreciated it. But this is a party, and not a wake. So let's celebrate the life we've got, and the joy we can find.''

Marty stepped off the risers and was lost to Emily's sight in the throng while the band took up a Bob Wills swing tune. Two couples got up to waltz and the buzz of conversation rose. Emily stood, stunned by the display of raw emotion she had just witnessed. Her star had a heart.

⋆ CHAPTER 3 ⋆

Emily crossed the expansive living room where now only a few couples sat, talking together on the cream-colored velvet sectional in front of the fireplace. As she entered the hall, she saw Anna coming out of the powder room.

"Did you hear that? His friend just died," Anna whispered. "He sounded so upset."

"I heard. I wonder when he found out. I guess that's why he was so quiet after the show. I wish he'd tell me these things. I never know what the man's thinking."

"You're better off not knowing what a man's thinking," Anna said, giving Emily's arm a motherly pat.

"Thanks for the advice, Dr. Ruth. Want to talk to me about sex?"

"No, but I probably should. I'll bet he'll need a lot of comforting tonight." Anna chortled and headed back toward the living room.

Emily walked past the powder room and turned down the hallway that lead to the master bedroom wing. As she passed Marty's study, she heard Tommy's voice.

"Oh, he's not going to come out of this one, I can guarantee that," Tommy said.

Emily stopped before she reached the open doorway.

"The rose is withering on the vine."

"I think you're underestimating his popularity, Tommy," said a male voice Emily didn't recognize. She leaned back against the wall and lifted one foot, pretending to examine the heel of her shoe.

"I'm telling you, he's not going to get this Nashville deal," Tommy went on. Emily could hear the clinking of ice cubes in a glass. "He's not mainstream. He's Branson, and you know those boys in Nashville aren't going to put their money over here. You just watch and see what happens."

"Going to be tough on you if he doesn't make it," the other voice said.

"Not the way I've got it planned." Emily heard Tommy's low chuckle.

"What do you mean?"

"I'm not talking about it now, but you watch and see. Going to be some changes around here, and ol' Tommy's going to have a little more cash flow real soon."

Emily heard rustling and turned back toward the living room. After a few steps, she stopped and listened. No one had come out of the room, so she walked purposefully back down the hallway. As she passed the study, she glanced in and saw Tommy leaning against a high-backed chair, his back toward the doorway. Facing Tommy and the doorway was a man Emily had seen a couple of times around town. She didn't know his name, but she remembered someone telling her he was a big shot from California, a money man who put deals together. Lately there were plenty of those types in Branson, so Emily had paid little attention. The man looked up and made eye contact with Emily as she passed the doorway. She wondered what the hell Tommy was up to. "Stop worrying," she told herself. "It's none of your business."

No one was in the study when she came out of the

bathroom. Outside, she saw Marty back at their table. In Emily's chair, a young woman was sitting, leaning across the table, her breasts nearly falling out of her silvery dress. She was deep in conversation with Marty. As Emily approached, she could hear the blonde telling Marty how quickly she picked up harmony.

"If you sing another number tonight, give me a try?" the woman asked, and Emily could have sworn she batted her eyelashes.

Marty stood when he saw Emily, and so did the young woman, without a glance at Emily.

"You come by the theater and see me next week, honey. We'll talk music," he told the woman with his best glowing smile.

"What can I get you, darlin'?" he asked as Emily sat down beside him.

"Who was that?"

"Everbody wants to back me, and my guess is this one's never even heard of Patsy Cline," he said.

"Your song was beautiful," Emily said, deciding to ignore the blonde who was laughing loudly nearby. She pulled her chair closer to Marty's. "I'm sorry about your friend. When did you find out?"

"Mom called me after the show tonight," he said. "He fell off the goddamned roof and broke his neck. He should have been up there onstage with me." Marty took a drink of his watery whiskey and motioned to a waiter.

"Want another *cerveza*?"

"*Por favor, señor*," Emily said.

"I'll take you to Cabo San Lucas this winter," Marty said, a shine coming back into his eyes. "We'll get us a little villa by the ocean, and you can drink *cervezas* all day, and we'll just lay on the sand."

"That would be so good," she said, hoping it would really happen. "You need a break. I'm glad you've got a couple weeks off."

"Well, I'm sure not getting a break this week. I'm supposed to be in Nashville Tuesday to talk to the big boys at TNN, and Chick's funeral's going to be Tuesday, Mom said."

The waiter brought the drinks. When he was gone, Marty took Emily's hand and looked at her earnestly.

"Take me to Mexico," Marty said. "Kidnap me, and we'll let them know where to send the royalty checks later."

"You know you don't want to do that," Emily said, deciding at that moment not to mention the conversation she overheard. "You can worry about all that tomorrow," she said, patting his hand. "It's your birthday, you've got a ton of presents, and"—she reached into her purse—"one from me."

Emily pulled out a small box, and Marty's eyes lit up as though he'd never been given a gift before.

"It's not much," Emily said.

Marty leaned over and kissed her softly on the lips.

"Thank you," he said seriously. "Whatever it is, it means more to me than anything could because I can already smell the love in here."

"Scented paper," she murmured as he tore off the wrapping.

Inside, a small photo album held pictures of all the good times they'd had over the past months. A photograph taken of them on their first date, an evening cruise on the *Table Rock Showboat* paddle wheeler. A picture of the couple the first night he'd had dinner at Emily's house with Rocko, Emily's Siamese, rubbing his leg. That was when Emily learned Marty was none too fond of cats.

Marty went through it page by page, laughing and commenting on all the fun they'd had. Emily warmed as she watched the happiness that showed on his face. When he came to the end, he put the album on the table, stood, and pulled her to her feet. He put his arms around her and held her close for a long moment.

"I don't know what I'd do without you, baby," he whispered. "No one's ever loved me better than you."

Emily savored the moment, but it was brief.

"All right, stop that smooching," Anna said. "I see you're opening presents. Let's get the Mack truck and bring out the rest of the loot."

Loot was the right word. Marty opened lavishly wrapped packages for the next forty-five minutes, calling out thank-yous to the people who gathered around the table. Many of the presents were in the rose motif. A small crystal rose paperweight, a ceramic rose-shaped teapot, a bouquet of roses formed from wood shavings. There was a martini set, a cordless drill—a gift from one of the stage crew—and the ugliest hand-painted necktie Emily had ever seen—a rose, of course.

Marty was gracious. And Anna oohed and aahed over each item, inspecting each one for labels and announcing details.

"This was handmade in Okinawa!"

At last, well after three, people began to leave. Anna came back from a slow waltz with Tommy.

"Well, we're going," she said, yawning. "I'm pooped. All I want to do is go home and get this dress off. But Tommy wants to go have breakfast." She made a face. "How can he think about breakfast after all the ribs I saw him eat?"

"Oh, he just wants to get you out in the car and fool around," Emily teased.

"He knows better than that. You just worry about your own chastity."

A few musicians were still playing softly when Marty whispered, "Come with me," and led Emily into the poolside cabana, away from the cool breeze that drifted across the lake. Through the open door, she could see the

bandstand and the rippling light reflecting from the pool.
He pulled her down beside him onto the wide lounger
and kissed her, the kind of long, soft kiss that made her
feel warm and safe and happy.

"You'll stay with me tonight?" he asked.

"I'll stay with you," she said.

"Meeting you was the luckiest thing that ever happened to me," he said, stroking her hair and neck. "Why
don't I go get us one champagne nightcap, and then we'll
just sneak away from the rest of them," he said, indicating the musicians.

"Hurry back," she said.

Marty left the cabana. Emily took off her shoes and
snuggled down into the soft cushions of the lounger. She
would have been excited about the coming events, but
she was so tired. She closed her eyes. In the moment
before she was deep asleep, she heard Marty singing an
old country song. In the background, a woman sang
slightly off-key.

⋆ CHAPTER 4 ⋆

Emily woke to the gentle prodding of Linn Yee, Marty's housekeeper.

"Good morning, Miss Stone," Linn said softly. "I've brought you some coffee and orange juice."

"What time is it?" Emily rose on one elbow. She was still wearing her sequins, but someone had covered her with a soft blanket. She blinked at the sunlight coming through the cabana door.

"It's nine thirty." Linn set a tray with a steaming mug of coffee and a tall glass of orange juice on the table beside the lounger. "Mr. Rose is in the living room, waiting for you. He said to tell you to take your time getting up. There are towels and everything you'll need in there," she said indicating the cabana's bathroom. "There are dressing gowns in a drawer in there, too, if you'd like to change."

Linn Yee stood waiting.

"Thank you, Linn," Emily said, pushing back her hair and sitting up. She felt a little embarrassed and wondered how many other women Linn Yee had provided with this gracious service. And what if she'd been in Marty's room? Probably a breakfast-in-bed routine.

"Can I do anything else?" asked the slight young woman.

"Thank you, no. Tell Marty I'll be up shortly."

Emily sat up and drank big gulps of the orange juice. She had a slight headache, and her neck was stiff. The dress was bunched around her waist and her pantyhose felt like they were painted on.

She stood up and stretched, took another drink of orange juice, and peeked through the cabana door. Outside, two men were picking up the remnants of last night's party. Emily walked into the bathroom and peeled off the dress and pantyhose. Her skin was pockmarked with sequin patterns.

She felt a slight sense of disappointment. Why hadn't Marty wakened her when he came in? She supposed it was gallant of him, picturing him kissing her tenderly and covering her with the throw. So making love with him was still ahead, something to look forward to. She also was relieved. She'd convinced herself that she was ready to take the plunge, but now that it hadn't happened, she was pleased that it was still optional. Emily had pretty traditional notions about sex. Although she didn't necessarily see marriage as a prerequisite, she couldn't imagine a one-night stand being fulfilling. Intimacy required friendship, and she wondered if she would feel his remoteness even when they were in bed.

When she had been married to Jim, they had been so close. They shared everything, all their feelings, fears, frustrations as well as joys. Making love seemed just an extension of that. Maybe she just wasn't ready for that yet with Marty. Passing out on the lounger might have been a stroke of luck.

Even here in the cabana, the bathroom was bigger than hers at home. On a shelf above the dressing table were stacks of pink towels. A basket on the countertop held small bars of soap and packets of shampoo, cream rinse, and body lotions—everything a guest might need. Emily pulled open one of the drawers in the dressing table and found it filled with swimming suits, all bikinis. She looked at sizes on two of the bottoms, a six and a ten. Nice of him to provide for a size ten. In the next drawer she opened, there were two silk robes in shades of pink. Beneath the robes were other pieces of lingerie. A lacey little black bodysuit with ties up the front, and a pair of turquoise blue sheer baby doll pajamas. Emily held the top up to her and looked in the mirror.

"Not in a million years, big guy," she said. If wedding bells ever rang and all this officially became her territory, the baby dolls would be the first thing to go. This was taking hospitality way too far. But since she couldn't picture trying to get back into the sequins, she picked out the longer of the two robes.

The shower felt wonderfully refreshing, even though there was only one showerhead. Twenty minutes later, her damp hair pulled back with a ribbon from the basket of barrettes and ties she had found in another drawer, Emily walked toward the house, the robe tightly sashed.

It was a beautiful morning, a hint of the day's heat already in the air. Marty was in the living room seated at a large glass-topped desk, his back to the door.

"I'll be there, Mom," he said. "I'll find a way. But it's at eleven o'clock? You're sure?"

Emily closed the door, and Marty looked around. He gave her a wave and motioned for her to sit at the table, where she saw a carafe and coffee cups.

"Okay. Of course. No, there's absolutely no need for you to go. It's a long drive. I know you still drive fine, but the whole town's going to be there. I'm sure Nita will understand, Mom. Okay. Bye."

He put down the phone and, just for a moment, squeezed his forehead with one hand as though willing away some pain.

"How's my sunshine this morning?" he asked, coming to stand behind her chair. He wrapped his arms around Emily's shoulders, and kissed her cheek. She could feel the roughness of his stubbly chin.

"Did you sleep okay?" he asked.

"Yes, except I've got marks all over me from the sequins. How'd I end up out there?"

"You went to sleep on me," he said. "Those ol' boys talked me into one last song with them, and by the time I got back with the champagne, you were out like a light."

Marty seemed distracted as he stacked up sections of the Sunday paper strewn on the couch.

"So I just covered you up and crept away. I thought I should wake you up and at least get that dress off of you, but I knew that wouldn't have been the end of it. And to tell you the truth, I was pretty bushed, too. When our time comes, I want it to be perfect."

"I know," Emily said. "It *will* be perfect, and I'm in no hurry."

"Well, I am," Marty said, coming back to the table. "It's those big, brown eyes of yours." He reached for her hand and kissed the back of it tenderly. After a moment, he released her hand and walked to the windows that overlooked the lake.

"Are you all right?"

"I'm fine. Just got so much on my mind, but it's nothing you have to hear about."

Emily recognized the tone of the martyr. She'd heard it often enough from her mother. Marty's body language, slumped shoulders, head hanging, made it clear he felt like an abandoned puppy. Emily couldn't stand it, so instead of keeping quiet, she went to him and slipped her arm around his waist and leaned her head against his shoulder.

"Tell me. Talk to me. Maybe I can help."

He turned to her and held her.

"Your hair smells like peaches," he said.

"You don't trust me at all, do you?" she said, pulling away from him.

"Of course I trust you, darlin'. Why would you say a thing like that?" He looked at her. "That's all I need right now is you getting upset with me."

"I'm not upset with you," she said in a defensive tone. She leaned back against the window frame and looked at his profile. She'd always treated him with kid gloves, just like everyone around Marty did. But that was too false, and she wanted a real relationship. She had to take the risk. If being honest with Marty ruined the relationship, it was better to know that now than find out later.

"It's just that you try to keep everything so bottled up inside that sometimes I feel like I don't even know you," Emily said gently. "And I want to know you. I want to know everything, the good or the bad. How else can I really feel close to you?"

He didn't move.

"You know, I'm not just some babe off the street. I care about you. I'd like to think that we've got something really special going, but how can I be everything I want to be to you if you keep me on the outside like some child looking in the candy store window?"

Without turning toward her, he took her hand and held it tightly.

"There's so much, Emily, so much I don't even like to think about."

He turned and walked to the sofa and sat heavily.

"Tuesday's the funeral of the only real friend I've ever had." He leaned back and stared at the ceiling. Emily went and sat beside him.

"People use me. I know it, and they know it. My life is all business. Even all the friendly folks here last night, hugging me, congratulating me on my birthday. How many of those people would still be around if I lost my voice, or I lost my theater? I don't believe Marty Rose would have a friend in the world."

"Surely you don't believe that," Emily said. "A lot of those people would stick with you and support you no matter what happened. You're a good person, you're creative, you're fun to be around, and I'm sure you've stuck by a lot of them when they've been having tough times. Besides, you're in no danger of losing either your voice or your theater."

"I wouldn't be so sure of that."

"Well, now you've got to explain that remark."

"Why? You want to check my bankbooks and see if I'm a good long-term prospect?"

"You're out of line, Marty," Emily said, anger tightening her voice. "I don't think I deserved that. Maybe I'd better just go home."

Marty was clearly taken aback.

"Oh, God, I'm sorry, honey." Marty turned to her and took her chin in his hand. "You're the best thing that's ever happened to me, and I love you so much. I'm just so full of troubles I don't know what to do. Please don't leave."

"I don't want to, but I don't want you to treat me like I'm the enemy."

"I know you're not."

Emily moved back so there was a little distance between them on the couch. "What did you mean about losing the theater?"

Marty got up and paced across the room, restless in contrast to the calm lake that stretched before him.

"When I built the Crystal Rose Theater ten years ago, there were only twelve other theaters in town," he said. "Now there are a lot more fingers in the pie, darlin'.' "

Emily was well aware of the overbuilding in Branson over the past few years. Before the boom, the peak season saw nearly every hotel room filled. There were waiting lines outside restaurants, and theater owners could count on sellout crowds most nights. But greedy developers had made that prosperity a thing of the past, at least for now.

"I'm an entertainer," Marty said, frustration raising his voice. "I'm not a businessman, so I counted on other people to make sure my books were in good shape, and that I could ride out whatever happened."

"I thought Tommy had been a good partner," Emily said. "Didn't he loan you some capital a couple of years ago?"

"Tommy came to me and offered me money," Marty said, picking at a hangnail. "I wish I'd never taken it."

"Why did you?"

"Because I wanted to do some things that the bankers didn't think I needed to do," Marty said. "Like buy a quarter-million-dollar crystal rose. But ol' Tommy was all in favor of it. Said how many people would come just to see it. Business was still pretty good then, so I signed him a two-year promissory note."

"I still don't understand," Emily said.

"The theater's the collateral," Marty said. "The note's due next month, and Tommy's made it very clear that if I don't pay him off, he'll sue me and foreclose on the theater."

"Could he do that? Doesn't the bank have a mortgage on it too?"

"Sure. But I've been paying off that mortgage for years. Tommy owns more of the theater than the bank does. And my guess is Tommy's got a silent partner with megabucks and a warehouse full of slot machines who can pay off the bank. Then Tommy's got himself a theater, and Marty's on the sidewalk. I realize now, too late, of course, that Tommy's been set from the start to screw me without so much as a kiss."

Emily was stunned. How could someone who takes in

as much money as a big entertainer does get himself into
such dire straits? Suddenly, the overheard conversation
at the party last night made a lot more sense.

As though reading her mind, Marty continued. "I'm
not selling as many tickets as I did a couple years ago.
I'm not selling as many souvenirs. I should have put the
crystal rose inside a building and charged tourists to take
pictures of it.".

"Won't the bank loan you enough to pay off
Tommy?"

"Do you think I'm too dumb not to have thought of
that?" Marty asked. He flopped into a chair across from
the sofa and pulled at the cording on the chair's arm.
"They're loaned out to the hilt over this building boom,
and they don't want to own any more theaters."

"So what about Zack? He's been your manager for so
long. Can't he help you out?"

"I'm not so sure Tommy and Zach don't have a little
deal working, too," Marty said, his voice hard and cold.
"Like I told you, I'm not sure who to trust anymore. All
I know is if I don't get this deal with TNN, I'm gone."

Emily pulled her robe together a little tighter at the
neck. They sat in silence for several moments.

"But even if he got the theater, why would he throw
you out?" Emily asked. "There isn't exactly a waiting
list of other stars who are dying to come to Branson,
certainly none that could fill your theater."

"I don't know exactly what he plans," Marty said.
"But I can smell a dead rat in his back pocket. You
know, the Crystal Rose could be turned into a mighty
fine casino."

"A casino!" Emily said, standing up to pace. "How
could he do that?"

"Honey, you can do anything you want with enough
money. Everything has a price."

"But the entire town would be up in arms. Everyone's

dead set against gambling here. How could he get away
with it?''

"Oh, Tommy wouldn't do it himself," Marty said.
"But I guarantee you, he knows the people who could.
Do you know how much money gambling brings in these
days? Billions. Billions and billions."

Marty watched her pacing. "Now I've got you all upset. That's why I didn't want to talk to you about this
crap. There's no reason why both of us should be
scared."

"I'm not scared," Emily said, stopping and putting her
hands in the pockets of the robe. "I have every confi-
dence that things will work out fine when you go to
Nashville. Branson's hot, and you're hot, and they'd be
fools to miss this opportunity to cash in on what their
competition's doing."

"I hope you're right, angel. But it's going to be a trick
Tuesday for me to be in two places at once."

"What do you mean?"

"I told you last night. Tuesday's the meeting in Nashville," Marty said, slouching lower in the chair. "I have
to be there. I absolutely do not trust Tommy and Zach to
handle this one for me. I've got to sell myself to the big
boys."

He scratched at the stubble on his chin.

"And I've got to be in Wimberley for Chick's funeral
at the same time." Emily heard a loon call somewhere
out on the lake, a plaintive wail, lonely as a train whistle
in the night but ending with the loon's trademark insane
laughing cry.

"Marty, I'm sure they'd understand if you couldn't go
to the funeral," Emily said. She sat back down on the
sofa across from his chair. "They know what a busy
schedule you have. Couldn't you just send a nice flower
arrangement and call his wife to explain you can't be
there?''

"You don't understand about Chick and me," Marty said, getting up and walking to an intercom on the wall. "I'm going to get Linn to make me a Bloody Mary. You want one?

"Why not? It's that kind of morning," Emily said.

After his instructions to Linn, Marty sat down on the sofa beside Emily. This is like being an old married couple, she thought. Me in my robe, Marty in his old sweats, talking about our troubles. Here in the mansion, she added to herself. She liked the feeling. Emily patted his knee, hoping she could somehow manage to lighten his mood.

"What don't I understand about Chick?"

Marty stared into space. Linn came in with two big Bloody Marys with salt on the rims, celery and limes on the silver tray beside the drinks. Marty reached for his silently.

"Thank you," Emily said to Linn. She picked up her glass. Linn nodded and left. Linn must know his moods better than I do, Emily thought. Marty stirred his drink with the stalk of celery. "Kids don't realize that every single thing they do is going to leave its mark on the rest of their lives," Marty said. *"I should have known, I should have known,"* he sang softly, a line from one of his songs that was a favorite of Emily's. "Tell me," Emily urged quietly.

"Without Chick, I'd be nothing. He handed me my first guitar, and taught me to play it. He started the Cadillac Cowboys, and dragged me to that little honky-tonk for our first gig. God, I was scared to death. But Chick had a real drive to be an entertainer back then. That year and a half that we toured the little towns around Wimberley, playing every juke joint that would have us, were the best years of my life."

Marty leaned forward, caught up in his story.

"Hell, we'd play for twenty-five dollars a night and

all the free beer we could drink. Did you ever see three drunk country boys try to split up twenty-five dollars?''

Marty laughed at the old memories.

"Who was the third Cadillac Cowboy?" Emily asked. There was a long silence.

"His name was Cole McCay." Emily could barely hear, Marty's voice was so low.

"What's happened to him?"

"I don't know. I don't want to know."

"So what happened to change things? Why didn't Chick stick with music?"

"Things happen," Marty said, still talking quietly like he was in a trance. "Things that change a man's heart. The night on Devil's Ridge changed his heart. And mine. It changed everything irreversibly and forever."

Emily sat wondering whether she should keep prodding. This seemed like a real sensitive subject, so she opted to keep quiet.

"And it was Nita, too," Marty continued, his voice rising to a normal tone. "Chick loved Nita from second grade on. And he was engaged to her by his senior year. She was real intent on having babies, and that started looking like a more stable future to him. I didn't have anybody, so the road drew me. If it hadn't been for Chick, I'd still be there in Wimberley, working at some convenience store or something. I'd never have been a teacher like he was. He was always smarter than me. But to fall off his roof. I can't believe he died in a stupid accident like that. I should have been there, like one of his neighbors, holding the ladder for him. Helping him."

Marty's voice broke, and Emily could see the tears welling up in his eyes.

"What's Devil's Ridge?" she asked, hoping to break the spell that had him so upset.

Marty squeezed his eyes with his hand. His breath quavered as he regained control. He looked at her steadily.

"Emily, I know you're trying to share some of my load, and I can't tell you how much it means to me. But there are some things in my past that need to stay buried. Devil's Ridge is one of those things. You've just got to understand. It's nothing that concerns you or us, and it's just got to stay in the past. I'm sorry I mentioned it."

"Your shrink would tell you to get everything out."

"A shrink did tell me that," Marty said, "but I've got some sense, even if it's backwards horse sense. I know that when you've faced evil, the last thing you want to do is call it back. I didn't mean to mention it now, and see? It's already causing trouble between us."

"It's not causing trouble between us," Emily said. "I sure don't want to cause you more pain. I was trying to help, but if you don't want to talk about it, that's okay. I don't need to see an instant replay of your life to know that you're a good man. I already know that. That's why I love you."

Marty put down his drink, and took Emily in his arms.

"Just stand by me," he said huskily.

"I will," she said, holding him tightly. "Just tell me how I can help. Maybe I could go to Wimberley as your representative to the funeral."

Marty pushed her back and looked at her with a faint, quizzical expression.

"No. You can't do that," he said.

"Why not? I could convey your desire to be there, and make a good case for why you couldn't. I know you're a wonder, but you really can't be in two places at once."

Marty stood up and stretched and looked down at Emily.

"You'd do that for me, wouldn't you?"

"Well, funerals aren't my favorite things, but it seems like it'd be better to have me there representing you than just to send flowers."

Marty walked to the windows.

"You're right," he said, turning to her. "It's a wonderful and generous idea, and I accept your offer. But you think about it today, and if you change your mind, I'll find some way to work it out."

"There isn't any other way," Emily said, already wishing she'd never thought of the idea. "It'll be fine. I'll get to see your hometown and meet some of the people you used to know. That'll be nice for me. And later, after the TNN show, we can go back down there together if you want to."

Marty came to the couch, and again wrapped her in a bear hug, rubbing her hip under the silky robe.

"Damn, girl, you're some kind of lady," he said. "I think maybe I'll carry you off for a while."

"No," said Emily pushing him back. "We've both got things to do today. I need to go home. If I'm flying off to Texas Tuesday, I've got to rework my schedule and get a lot done this afternoon. And you've got a lot to do, too."

"Are you always going to be right, or do I get to be right once in a while?" Marty's smile eased her apprehension about the trip to Texas.

"Have you got a spare pair of sweats I can borrow?" Emily asked. "I'm not walking up to my house in this kimono, and I sure don't want to try to squeeze myself back into those sequins this morning."

"You were the most beautiful girl at the party last night."

"Well, fix me up, and I'll be the most beautiful girl in your sweats." Again it crossed Emily's mind to wonder how many other younger, more glamorous women had shared Marty's closet. But she quickly resolved that she'd never ask about that. Maybe intimacy did have its limits.

Marty went to the intercom. "Could you have John bring the limo up? Miss Emily's ready for a ride home."

"Come on in here, and take your pick," Marty said. Emily followed Marty to the closet adjoining his bedroom. It looked like the men's department at Marshall Fields.

"Geez, Marty. You just don't have a thing to wear," she joked.

"If they don't like me in Nashville, honey, I might be left with nothing but the shirt on my back."

Emily loved the rumble of his laugh, and she was glad to see him cheerful again. She picked out a pair of sweats, happy to see there were none in petite sizes or pastel shades.

"These okay?" she asked.

"Whatever you want," he said, leaning in the doorway.

"Out," she said, pushing him gently and closing the door in his face. She had to roll up the waist and cuffs, but the effect was certainly more acceptable than the alternative.

"Well, aren't you cute," he said when she came out. "Want to borrow a pair of my boots? Walk a mile in my moccasins?"

"No thanks," she said. "Are you coming too?"

"No, I'll let John take you home. I need to get cleaned up and go on over to the theater. Shuffle papers for a while, and try to make sure my ducks are lined up for Nashville."

"You'll go worry for awhile, you mean?"

"You're getting to know me too well," he said. "You think about your offer. Your stock won't drop if you change your mind."

At the door, Marty kissed her slowly and sweetly.

"You're the best, baby."

Marty's driver pulled up in front of the house.

"You didn't need to get the limo out," Emily said as Marty opened the rear door for her. "I wouldn't have minded riding in the little old Blazer."

"Nothing but the best for my lady." He leaned into the spacious backseat and kissed her on the cheek.

"You have a nice day," he said, and closed the door.

After all they'd been through that morning, his final "have a nice day" left an impression of cold formality. Maybe it's me, she thought. I need to be patient and adjust to his lifestyle. As the limo rounded the far curve on the road, Emily looked back at the mansion, barely visible now through the woods. The king was alone in his castle.

✮ CHAPTER 5 ✮

Emily loved the old Victorian house she'd bought in Branson. The octagonal-shaped rooms on either side of the spacious entry hall gave the place a special charm. And the big yard with lots of old oak trees and beds of flowers gave her a feeling of privacy. This spring, her mother had hired Gordon Anderson to till a garden spot. Anderson was a jack-of-all-trades who lived just up the quiet street. Anna often spent Sundays on her knees, not in church but in her garden. Already there were tomatoes beginning to redden on the vine, and eight varieties of tiny peppers from bells to habeneros dangled on the young plants.

"They're so hot you don't even touch them without gloves," Anna had warned.

"So how are we supposed to eat them?" Emily wanted to know.

As the limo pulled up to the curb, Emily saw a late-model black Cadillac parked in front of the house. Tommy Jamison, his mirrored sunglasses gleaming, leaned out of the driver's side window and waved. As John came around to let her out, Emily saw Anna emerge from the passenger side of the Cadillac. She was still wearing her green dress from the night before.

"Thanks for everything," Anna called to Tommy. "I'll see you soon."

She and Emily met on the front stairs.

"Good morning, Emily," Anna said quietly.

"Good morning," Emily said. Both women felt embarrassed to be caught coming home in the morning from all-night interludes with boyfriends, not the standard mother-daughter meeting.

"Been to church?" Emily asked, indicating Anna's dressy attire.

Simultaneously, both women fell into peals of laughter as the Cadillac and the limo pulled away.

Anna leaned against the stone wall, laughing until tears rolled down her cheeks. She calmed down, then noticed how Emily was dressed and broke up again.

"All right," Emily finally managed, rummaging in her purse for the house key. "I think the two old floozies better go inside. Would you mind holding my dress?" That started the laughter again.

Inside, Anna set the dress and shoes on the hall table and tried to catch her breath.

"Oh, God," she said. "I never thought my daughter would catch me sneaking into the house."

"Believe me," said Emily, dabbing at tears, "it's about the last thing I ever thought *I'd* see!"

Emily got a bottle of Evian water from the refrigerator while Anna went to change clothes.

When Anna came back, now comfortable in a rumpled, pilly navy sweatsuit, the two sat at the patio table beneath a flowered umbrella.

"So did you have a good time?," Emily asked. "What did you do after you left the party? And, more to the point, where did you sleep?"

"Oh, now stop it," Anna said, stirring a cup of instant coffee from the microwave. "I didn't do anything."

"Yeah, that's what I used to tell you, and you never

believed me, either,'' Emily said.

"Well, that was a little different. I was in the good hands of the richest man I've ever known. We went to the Farmhouse, and met some other people there. I felt like a fifth wheel with Tommy talking about all his big business deals. He's so intent on impressing people.''

Rocko strolled onto the patio, rubbed Emily's leg, and leapt to the table, lecturing them in his raspy cat voice.

"See? Even Rocko doesn't approve of our lifestyle,'' Emily said.

"There's nothing wrong with it,'' Anna said. "We just run with a fast crowd.''

"So what'd you do after the Farmhouse?'' Emily asked. "You still haven't said where you slept.''

"Well, neither have you. You first,'' Anna said.

"I slept on the lounger in Marty's cabana,'' Emily said, rubbing her neck. "He was still playing with the band, and I just fell asleep.''

"Well, I slept on Tommy's couch with him snoring beside me,'' Anna said. "Tommy wanted to show me some photos of a big piece of land he's trying to buy, so we stopped by his house after breakfast. It must have been four thirty by then. I think we both fell asleep at the same time.''

"Is his house lavish?'' Emily asked.

"Not really,'' Anna said. "He's got nice things, but the place obviously could use a woman's touch to make it more homey.''

"Want to be that woman?''

Anna thought about it.

"I don't know. Sometimes I think maybe it'd be nice to live with a man again. I've been on my own for twenty years, and the pickings are getting slimmer. And Tommy's got enough money so I wouldn't have to worry about anything.''

"Yeah, nothing but how to put up with him for the

rest of your life,'' Emily said.

"I know,'' Anna said. "I like his companionship, but I just don't feel serious about this. I'll give it a while. Sometimes I'm not even sure how much I like Tommy. What about you? Did Marty propose last night?''

"Oh, I think it'll be a long time before Marty proposes marriage to anyone,'' Emily said. "And I'm certainly not ready to say yes if he did.''

Anna pushed the noisy cat off the table. "Hush, Rocko.''

"Sometimes Marty's so distant,'' Emily said. "This morning, I tried to get him to tell me about some of the things that have been bothering him lately. And now I kind of wish I'd never asked.''

Suddenly Emily stopped herself. She didn't want to tell Anna about Marty's troubles with Tommy. Maybe Marty was overreacting to think Tommy was trying to ruin him, although after the conversation she'd overheard last night she tended to concur with Marty's appraisal. She just didn't want to give in to the petty temptation to gossip when that's all it would be at this point.

"Why? What'd he say?'' Anna asked.

"Well, he's worried that if he doesn't get the TNN deal, he could be in financial trouble.''

"How could he be in financial trouble? What's he been spending his money on?'' Anna asked.

"He spared no expense on that theater and the gardens and all, the crystal rose, and now with the added competition, it's a cash flow problem,'' Emily said. "I don't really understand how it could have happened either. And he's all upset over his friend Chick's death. This is where I got myself in trouble.''

"What kind of trouble?''

"Well, I hate to admit this,'' Emily said, "but I offered to fly to Texas Tuesday and go to the funeral as his representative.''

"Why'd you do that?" Anna said. "You hate funerals."

"I didn't think about it before I offered," Emily said. "I was just trying to make him feel better. And I didn't think he'd accept."

"Are you going through with it?"

"I have to now," Emily said. "Besides, maybe it'll be fun to see a part of Texas I've never visited."

A sudden call of "Hello, ladies" startled them both as Gordon Anderson rounded the corner of the house. "How's everyone this morning?" he boomed cheerfully.

He picked Rocko up from a chair and put him on the ground, much to Rocko's disgust. "Mind if I join you, or is this girl talk?"

Gordon Anderson was the best kind of good old boy. He'd lived in Branson all his life, and remembered when the town was a small stop on the railroad line and the only tourists were fishermen. Gordon had worked for the railroad for twenty years as the ticketmaster, but had never taken advantage of the free ride he could have had to just about anyplace. In fact, he was proud to say he'd never left Missouri.

"Why would I want to go anywhere else?" he had asked Emily when she expressed astonishment at his lack of wanderlust. She had no answer to his question.

Gordon's wife Sophie had died more than a decade ago, and he still lived in the small home they'd shared just up the street from Emily's house. Emily met Gordon the day she moved in. He'd come down to see if he could help the movers with anything. He'd known the last people to live in the house, and he knew every defect in the house, too.

"You'll be needing a new water heater, and come fall, you'll need someone to help you with those old storm windows. They're real heavy," he'd warned.

Within ten minutes, Gordon had convinced Emily that

the thing she needed most in the world was a good handyman. Now, he was indispensable. He'd do anything for a person he liked, he was fiercely loyal, and he moved as slow as a snail. Emily thought of him as her favorite uncle.

He was a slight man, short and thin except for a potbelly that nearly covered the wide leather belt he always wore. His thinning gray hair was always neatly slicked back, and his teeth were white despite the cigars Emily sometimes saw him puffing as he sat in the swing on his front porch. He'd never smoked a cigar around Emily or Anna, perhaps conditioning thanks to Sophie.

And Anna liked Gordon, too. She could argue with him until she was blue in the face without offending him. Some mornings Emily would hear them on the patio wrangling over the latest political issue. Sometimes he and Anna would play pinochle for hours. Before Anna had met Tommy, Emily had suggested she might be interested in Gordon.

"Ha!" Anna had crowed. "What would I want with some poor old hill boy that's never even see the ocean?"

This was ironic since Emily's father had been a poor old hill boy to whom Anna had been happily married for sixteen years until his death when Emily was ten years old. But her father had, indeed, seen the ocean. And he'd been self-educated and wise. Gordon didn't have that kind of polish. Still, Emily thought Gordon was more suited for her mom than Tommy Jamison.

"So, did you girls have fun last night at the fancy shindig?" Gordon asked.

"Yes," Emily said. "Get Mom to tell you all about it. I'm going to go see if I have anything to wear to a funeral. By the way, Gordon, are you going to get the rest of my cabinets up this week, so I can restore some kind of order in my kitchen?"

"I'd think so," Gordon said.

It must be a country thing to be so vague with your answers, Emily thought. Gordon seemed to hedge about everything. "I couldn't rightly say," was one of his stock replies.

"Who died?" Emily heard Gordon asked as she went inside, Rocko weaving between her legs and talking to her as she went upstairs to her bedroom.

Emily took off the warm-up suit and slipped on shorts and a T-shirt, pleased to see that the sequin markings had disappeared from her waistline. She opened her closet and began mentally packing. She found the black dress she'd had in mind and thought it would be suitable despite the lacey collar. At least it was sleeveless, and Emily could imagine how hot it could be this time of year in south central Texas.

After she laid out the dress and other items she would need on her bed, she took down an atlas and turned to Texas. There, south of Austin, she found Wimberley. She had to squint to see it, and reminded herself to replace the reading glasses she had broken last week. After a brief search, Emily located her big magnifying glass on the desk in her office under some papers.

Back on her bed, she lay on her stomach and examined the map more closely. Just south of the dot called Wimberley was an even smaller dot. "Devil's Ridge."

"That looks like a nice little side trip," she said to Rocko. "I wonder if I'll find the devil."

⋆ CHAPTER 6 ⋆

When Emily walked into Marty's spacious office above the theater just before noon on Monday, she was hoping he had changed his mind about her trip to the funeral the next day. The door to Marty's inner office was closed, a signal Emily knew meant Do Not Disturb.

"Hi, Tammy," Emily said. Tammy was cradling the phone on her shoulder. Three other people were sitting in the outer office, apparently waiting to see Marty. Two were obviously salesmen, their hefty briefcases beside them. The other person was the blond wannabe singer who had cooed over Marty at the party.

"What time do you want to leave for Austin tomorrow morning?" Tammy asked. "You can leave at five twenty and get in there at eight thirty, or you can wait and leave at six fifteen, but there's a longer layover in St. Louis and you wouldn't get into Austin until nine forty. The funeral's at eleven, and Marty said it's about an hour's drive to Wimberley, so by the time you get your bags and pick up the rental car, the later flight's really cutting it too close, so how about the flight at five twenty in case you have car trouble or get lost?"

"Five twenty!" said Emily, not quite following Tammy's discourse.

"We'll go with the five twenty flight," Tammy said into the phone. "Then coming back Wednesday, we'll take the two P.M. flight."

"Can't I come back Tuesday after the funeral?" Emily asked.

"Thank you," Tammy said, hanging up the phone.

"Why can't I fly back Tuesday?" Emily asked again.

"Because the only other flight Tuesday leaves at three in the afternoon. You'll have to go from the service at the church to the cemetery, and then everyone will get together for a meal," Tammy said. "You won't be through with all of that until after three. If you left early, it would look rude."

"Can't I fly out earlier on Wednesday?" Emily asked, growing annoyed.

"I thought maybe you'd want to sleep late," Tammy said. "You'll be tired. I can call back and change it if you want me to."

Emily sighed. "No, it's okay. I probably will want to sleep in. I don't imagine there's much else to do in Wimberley."

"Go visit the birthplace of Marty Rose," Tammy said. "I hear it's a shrine."

At first Emily thought she was being serious, but then she saw Tammy's grin.

"Little joke," Tammy said.

Emily wasn't sure how to react. It was the first time Tammy had kidded with her. She glanced at the office door.

"Has he got someone in there?" Emily asked.

"Tommy," Tammy said. "He just got here. Marty said to hold his calls. I don't know what's going on. Do you want to wait in the Faded Rose? I'll tell him you're there as soon as he gets through."

"I guess so," Emily said. "Can I take this?" she

asked, picking up a copy of *USA Today* that lay on Tammy's desk.

"Sure," Tammy said. "You get breakfast on the plane tomorrow."

"Oh, good," Emily said as she left the office.

In the inner office, Marty sat behind his desk. His face was pale. Tommy was pacing.

"I can't believe it," Tommy said. "Zach's dead? How'd you find out?"

"That weasel Fred Bundy called me as soon as he heard Zach had been killed to tell me I needed a new agent. A real nice way to find out."

"What happened to him?" Tommy asked.

"All I know is that his secretary found him dead this morning. He was lying in a pool of blood beside his desk. Fred said he'd been shot in the chest three times. They think it happened Friday night. Who do you know that would want to kill Zach?"

"A lot of people," Tommy said. "I heard he was running up some pretty serious gambling debts."

"Gambling?" Marty said. "I didn't know he was into that? Horses?"

"No." Tommy straightened a photo on Marty's wall. "He took a lot of trips to Biloxi lately, to the casinos there. High-stakes poker, I heard."

"Jesus, I thought Zach was smarter than that. See what your gambling's done?"

"Hey, it's not my gambling." A pink flush of anger rose in Tommy's cheeks. "If someone's going to gamble, they'll find a way to do it, casinos or not. I don't know why you refuse to wise up. You think the governor's going to stick to his high moral rhetoric and turn down billions in revenue once he gets reelected next year? Someone's going to get gambling in here, and it might as well be us leading the crowd. Sooner or later, everyone will want a piece of the action."

"Yeah, and they can get a bullet in the chest as a bonus," Marty said. He rubbed his face. "When did you see Zach last?"

Tommy stopped pacing and glowered at Marty. "What kind of goddamned question is that? We were both in Nashville last week. When did you see him last?"

"I didn't see him. I played the fair and that was it. You were the one that said you wanted to stay."

"So when did you come back?"

"I flew back Thursday night, just like I said I was going to. When did you come back?"

"Saturday morning," Tommy said. "I bumped into Phil Harmon Friday and he was coming back, so I hopped on his plane. You can ask him."

"Yeah, but when did you last see Zach?"

"What are you now, a prosecuting attorney?" Tommy asked, his voice rising.

"Keep it down," Marty said. "You want everyone out there to hear us?"

"What are you implying?" Tommy came to the desk and leaned on it with his fists. "That I killed him? That I pumped bullets into Zach? You've lost it, Marty."

"How would I know what went on with you and Zach? You've seen more of my agent this year than I have."

"Well, if anyone was a suspect here, it'd be you," Tommy said menacingly. "You've got a lot more reason to want him dead than I would."

"What the hell do you mean by that?" Marty stood up quickly, his leather chair rolling away behind him.

"Goddammit, Marty, I don't mean anything by it," Tommy raised his palms innocently as he took a step back from the desk. "It's just the shock of this whole thing. Ten to one it was something to do with his gambling, or some client he was cheating."

"Are you saying Zach was cheating me?"

"Who knows? Could be a million things we didn't know about Zach's business."

"So when did you see him last?" Marty asked evenly.

"I saw him Friday," Tommy said. "We had lunch downtown, I walked him back to the office, and we said goodbye. People saw me Friday night. I've got plenty of alibis, not that anyone but you would ask."

"What'd you talk about Friday?" Marty asked, watching Tommy closely.

"What do you think we talked about?" Tommy snapped. "We talked about you and our chances of getting TNN. Zach thought the chances were good if we'd be willing to deal. You know, we have to be smart about this meeting tomorrow."

"*We* aren't going to be at the meeting tomorrow," Marty said. Small muscles twitched in his jaws. "This is *my* deal, and *I'll* be meeting with TNN tomorrow. Let's not forget what the product is here. I don't need your help to sell Marty Rose. I've been selling Marty Rose for thirty years, and I've done a real fine job of marketing. And don't forget whose theater you're in." Marty's voice rose. "Those people in the lobby aren't buying tickets to see Tommy Jamison."

"Well, in case you didn't look this morning, there aren't too many people in the lobby buying tickets," Tommy said, stabbing his finger toward Marty. His face was beginning to match the burgundy sofa. "If it wasn't for me, you'd be performing out of the back of a pickup truck down at the mall right now. And you can go buy the pickup when TNN tells you to kiss their ass tomorrow."

"You get the hell out of my office, you son of a bitch," Marty said in a low growl. "You don't own me, and you never will."

"Fine," Tommy said, jerking open the office door.

"You have a good time in Nashville tomorrow. I hear they've got Chevys on sale." He slammed the door.

Emily knew something was wrong the moment Marty came into the coffee shop. His face was flushed, his lips tightly set. He headed for her booth in the back, but was stopped by a couple who held out their menu for him to autograph.

Marty smiled his good smile. Emily watched him talking to them, laughing, signing his name. The expression of pleasure died the moment he turned away.

"What's happened?" she asked as he sat down.

"Coffee," he barked to the waitress halfway across the room.

"Zach's dead," Marty told her quietly.

"No," Emily said, shocked. "What happened?"

They waited while the waitress brought Marty's coffee and refilled Emily's cup.

"Another agent called me this morning," Marty said. "His secretary found him in his office. He was shot, they think Friday night." Marty recounted most of the his conversation with Tommy, the anger coming back into his face.

"First Chick, now Zach," Marty said grimly. "I don't know what's going to go wrong next."

"Well, nothing's going wrong in Nashville tomorrow, and I'll be fine in Texas," Emily reassured him. She took his hand across the table. "Just keep your cool."

"Marty Rose'll be just fine," he said with determination. "It doesn't matter what Zach and Tommy were up to. This won't be the first contract I've negotiated, and it won't be the last."

Emily had wanted to ask Marty more about Wimberley and the people she would meet there, but she could see how distracted he was.

"I've got a lot of things to do today, and I know you

do too," she said. "Why don't you come over tonight when you're ready for a break, and we'll relax for a while. I could challenge you to a game of Scrabble," she said, trying to sound playful.

"All right," Marty said, swallowing the last of his coffee and waving off the waitress. "Tammy get you all set on the plane tickets?"

"Yes," Emily said. "I leave at five thirty."

"Tonight?" Marty asked as he stood up.

"No. In the morning," Emily said slowly, realizing he hadn't been paying attention. "That means you can't keep me up late tonight."

"When do you get back?"

"Wednesday evening," Emily slid out of the booth. "When are you coming back?"

"It just depends on how things go. If they go bad, it may be my last trip on the Scooter," he said, referring to his private jet. He gave her a hug around her shoulders. "I'll see you later," he said, and strode out of the coffee shop.

On the drive home, Emily couldn't get the image of Zach out of her mind. She'd never met Marty's agent, but there was a photo of him with Marty hanging in Marty's office. It was turning into a grim week, and she worried about what Marty might walk into when he arrived in Nashville.

At home, Emily found Anna taking a nap in a recliner in the living room, snoring softly. Emily finished packing and tidied up the kitchen. But she kept thinking of Zach. She went to the rolodex on her desk and dialed the *Tampa Tribune* newsroom.

"Chris?" Emily said. "It's Emily Stone. How have you been?"

After a few minutes of catching up with her old friend who had long covered the entertainment scene in Tampa, Emily broached the reason for her call.

"I was wondering if you have any contacts at TNN? What I need is someone I could chat with confidentially, just to see if there's any talk about a TNN deal with Marty Rose. He's an entertainer here in Branson, and we've heard rumors he's cooking up a television special. I'm just nosing around a little. Yeah, I guess. Once a reporter, always a reporter."

When Emily had the name and phone number she wanted, she hung up, and sat for a few minutes, debating whether or not to make the call. What if her call somehow got back to Marty? He might be angry that she was poking into his business. On the other hand, if there were any rumors or talk about the impending deal, Emily's knowledge might either forewarn him or encourage him. She placed the call.

"Hello. Is Ellen Browning there?" Emily tapped her fingers nervously while she waited, planning what she would say. When a pleasant-sounding woman answered, Emily explained how she'd gotten Ellen's name, and that she was a freelance writer in Branson who was checking on a rumor about Marty Rose and TNN.

"I know you can't give out any inside information, but I was just wondering if there's any talk about this at TNN?"

"Can we talk off the record?" the woman asked. "I wouldn't want to be quoted on this. If they make a deal, I'll be issuing a press release, but officially I can't say anything yet."

"That's fine," Emily assured her. "I'm not writing about this, but I do like to keep up with what's happening here."

"Well, as long as you won't quote me, I don't think it's any secret that TNN's interested in signing Marty Rose for a special, and maybe even a regular show. I'm just one of several people in public relations, so I'm not on the inside of anything, but I have heard that some of

the execs were waiting to get some tapes of Rose's shows
and were annoyed that he hadn't responded to their re-
quests. Have you heard about his agent, Zach Zimrest?''

Emily hadn't been ready for this line of conversation,
so she pleaded ignorance and astonishment while Ellen
recounted the morning's discovery.

"Who do they think did it?" Emily asked.

"The noon news said the police are 'following several
leads,' but that usually means they don't know anything
yet. Someone here said they thought he was into gambling, but I also heard he had a big, noisy fight a couple
of weeks ago out in a restaurant with another singer he
represents who accused Zimrest of skimming money
from his accounts. I even heard rumors he was involved
in some kind of drug deal, but who knows what these
high rollers do," Ellen said. "I'm sorry I couldn't be
more help to you."

Emily thanked Ellen for the information and hung up.
The only thing she'd learned of any possible value to
Marty was that TNN hadn't gotten tapes they'd wanted
from Marty. She wondered whose mistake that had been.
Probably Zach's. Marty should know, and Emily resolved
to think of some story about how she had heard this and
tell Marty about it tonight.

Emily spent the afternoon and evening avoiding con-
versations with Anna by keeping her nose in a book. She
didn't want to have to tell Anna any of these allegations
about Tommy or Zach unless it became absolutely necessary. And she knew Anna was looking forward to dinner with Tommy tonight. At seven, she told Anna to have
a good time, then left the room before Tommy arrived to
pick up Anna.

When Marty hadn't called by nine, Emily left a message on his home and office answering machines. By ten,
Emily began to get angry. Here she was all packed, ready
to spend two days of her time doing him a favor, and he

couldn't take time to call her. Emily called again at ten
thirty. She could tell from the number of beeps on his
answering machines that he hadn't taken his calls or
checked his messages. This was so irresponsible of him,
and it wasn't the first time Marty had said he'd stop by
later and hadn't showed. And it wasn't the first time he'd
not returned her calls. Then she remembered the last time
it had happened. She'd expected to hear from him last
Friday when he'd returned from playing the Tennessee
State Fair the day before. But he hadn't called until Saturday morning. They'd been so busy talking about the
benefit show that night, she hadn't bothered to quiz him
about his whereabouts Friday night. Suddenly Emily
wondered if Marty was in more trouble than she realized.
Impossible. She'd seen the look of shock on his face this
afternoon when he'd told her about Zach's death. Emily
imagined Marty out with some pal right now, talking
about the business in Nashville. Maybe he'd gone to
sleep early. Wherever he was, he'd obviously forgotten
about her. Damn, she thought, why couldn't he be more
thoughtful. It could be such a nice relationship. Well, I'll
go through with the trip, but that's it for Mrs. Nice Guy.
Next week, I'll get things straightened out with him. I
don't care how much his fans adore him. Either he treats
me with respect, or he can take a hike. The hell with
limousines.

✳ CHAPTER 7 ✳

It was a quarter after nine Tuesday morning when Emily turned off Interstate 35 at San Marcos and headed toward Wimberley. It had taken her a little extra time to get out of the Austin traffic, but she'd be there in plenty of time to find a motel and change into her funeral clothes. She'd hardly thought of the funeral, focusing instead on Marty's fate in Nashville today. She was still irritated that he hadn't called her last night. She had wanted to forewarn him that TNN might have been given a bad impression about his interest in doing the show. But in the final analysis, it was his problem. All he needed to do was sign that TNN contract and his troubles would be over. At least, until he had to tangle with Emily.

So far, the drive had been uneventful. She wondered if Marty would have suggested renting a limousine, but he hadn't offered her spending money for the trip, so she'd opted for economy. She certainly wasn't going to give him a bill for the trip. Besides, there was no reason to attract undue attention to herself by showing up in a fancy car.

The scenery reminded her of the Ozarks. Big oak trees and cedars sheltered the rolling hills and rocky outcroppings. Small farms and unpretentious houses dotted the landscape. Heading out Route 12 could have been the drive to her own hometown of Blue Eye. Emily warmed to the idea that she and Marty came from similar roots. Maybe she was being too hard on him just because he wasn't as reliable as she thought he should be. She wondered what Marty's mother was like. She passed a sign that read: "WIMBERLEY—6 MILES." She began to watch for signs advertising motels and resorts. Judging by the billboards, there were more churches in town than anything else.

The town square was charming with quaint little gift shops, antiques stores, and a couple of appealing restaurants. She drove around the square, then headed east, following signs to the Wimberley Inn Motel. It looked neat and clean, and the desk clerk was pleasant, so Emily checked in. She hung up her clothes, shaking the wrinkles out of the black crepe dress. She was glad it was sleeveless. It was already hot. "Dry heat" had never seemed any cooler to Emily.

Since it was only ten, Emily decided she'd change and then go back to the square and look around. She could ask someone there for directions to the Thompson Funeral Home. She found a parking place in front of the Cypress Creek Cafe and went inside where it was cool and dark. There were only a few people finishing breakfast. She had barely seated herself in a booth when a plump, middle-aged waitress came over bringing ice water, a menu, and a basket of chips. A bowl of salsa was already on the table.

"How y'all doing today?" the woman asked. Her name tag said she was Sally.

"I'm fine," Emily said.

"You need some time to decide?"

"I'll just have a cup of coffee," Emily said.

When Sally brought the coffee, Emily asked her if she could tell her how to get to Thompson's Funeral Home.

"You here for Chick's funeral, are you?" Sally asked.

"Yes. How'd you guess that?"

"Because we don't have too many funerals in a town this small, thank the Lord. Where'd you come in from?"

"I drove from Austin this morning," Emily said.

"You a friend of Chick and Nita?"

This was pushing neighborly curiosity, but after all, Emily had come representing Marty, a hometown boy, so she decided this was as good a time as any to let the word out that Marty wasn't coming. And she figured Sally was just the girl to do it.

"Actually, I'm here representing Marty Rose. He was a good friend of Chick's, but he couldn't make it today, so I came to offer his condolences."

Sally was momentarily silent.

"He's an entertainer up in Branson, Missouri, but he grew up here," Emily explained.

"Oh, I know who Marty is," Sally said, seating herself in the booth across from Emily. "How's Marty doing up there? I keep promising myself to get up to Branson, but I haven't yet. I hear it's quite a place now. He got a big, fancy theater?"

"Yes. It's a beautiful theater. You ought to come visit. Did you know Marty?"

"Sure, I knew him," Sally said. "I was three grades behind him in high school, but I had a crush on him like all the other girls did." She grinned. Either she hadn't aged well, or the information about being younger was a small fantasy on Sally's part. Emily didn't care. She just wanted directions to the funeral home.

"Is Thompson's close to the square?" she asked, trying to remind Sally of the original question.

"Well, yes, it's just out on River Road, but the funeral's been postponed."

"Postponed? Why?" Emily wondered why no one had notified Marty.

Sally leaned across the table, put one hand up beside her mouth, and whispered, even though by then they were the only two in the room.

"There's going to be a coroner's inquest." Sally nodded knowingly, then looked around the dining room. "They can't bury him until they find out if there was *foul play*."

"Foul play?" Emily whispered back. "I thought he fell off his roof."

"Everyone did," Sally said, dropping her hand and taking up a more normal tone. "See, here's what happened."

Here comes the intrigue, Emily thought with anticipation. She could see the eagerness for the retelling in Sally's eyes.

"Nita, that's his wife, well, I guess you know that, had been off at a training conference for county clerks. She's the county clerk, you know. She left on Wednesday and didn't come home until Saturday. That's when she found him." Her voice dropped again to a whisper. "He was lying there in the yard, dead as a doornail, right in the flower bed. And there was a ladder up on the roof and a bucket of tar where he'd been fixing around the chimney. They must have had a little leak. That happens sometimes with the hailstorms we get here. Chick was a teacher, you know, so he was out of school for the summer."

Sally drummed her fingernails on the table.

Emily encouraged Sally to continue. "Do they have a nice house?"

"Well, it's not so much, but he always had it kept real nice, pretty flowers in the yard and all. Anyway, when Nita got back, there he was. Everyone figured he lost his balance up there on the roof and hit his head on that brick edging on the flower bed. I guess Nita was just fit to be tied to think of him being up there on that roof with her not even in the house. Men can be the biggest fools."

She stopped drumming her nails as though finished with the account.

"So why are they having an inquest?" Emily prompted.

"Oh. Well, I guess the coroner found something wrong when he was examining him."

"But why postpone the funeral?"

"I heard they're sending his body up to Austin for some kind of tests," Sally said, drumming again. "We think it might just be the coroner trying to make himself look real thorough, you know? He's up for reelection this year."

Emily pictured Zach in a pool of blood. "They don't think he was killed, do they?" she asked.

"Oh, no," Sally said, wagging her head. "I can't imagine anyone would want to kill the poor man." She scratched her chin as she pondered the idea. "Maybe some student who had a grudge against him. You know how students are these days, guns at school and everything."

"Surely not in Wimberley," Emily said.

Sally poked some stray hairs back into the bun atop her head. "It's a shame, but this town's growing, and there are people moving in here from all over the country. Those new kids are different, you know? Not raised like the kids that was born here. You never know what can happen anymore with bombings and killings everywhere."

Emily wasn't interested in Sally's social commentary. "When is the inquest?"

"Well, I don't know, but I do know there's no funeral today. Looks like you had a long trip for nothing. You a good friend of Marty's?"

Apparently, Sally thought it was her turn now to ask the questions.

"I'm a friend," Emily said. She scooted to the edge

of the booth and stood up to indicate to Sally that she'd like to leave now.

But Sally didn't make a move to leave the booth.

"He's not married yet, is he?"

"No." Now Emily pulled money out of her wallet, but that seemed to have no effect either.

"I always wondered why he never married," Sally mused. "Such a good looker, and must be loaded by this time. He got a steady girl?"

"Yes," Emily said. "He is seeing someone. I guess I'd better pay up and get on my way."

Sally began to slowly pull herself out of the booth, taking her sweet time about it.

"You his secretary?" she asked as she picked up Emily's coffee cup.

"No," said Emily, deciding to put a halt to this. "I'm his girlfriend."

"Oh, now, isn't that nice," said Sally, her eyebrows raised. She gave Emily a more appraising look. "Too bad you couldn't have come down together. Lots of nice honeymoon cabins over along the river."

Emily didn't take the bait and said nothing else until Sally, who seemed to be temporarily out of questions, handed her the change.

"Well, you have a nice stay in Wimberley," Sally said. "Come back in for dinner. We've got a special on the ribs tonight."

"Thanks. Maybe I will," Emily turned to go, then stopped. "By the way, do you know how to get to Devil's Ridge?"

Sally's smile disappeared. "Why would you want to go out there?"

"I just heard that's a nice scenic drive," Emily said. She was intrigued by Sally's apparent change of mood.

"It's out on Route 32, over in Comal County," Sally said slowly, "but there's really nothing there. Just a windy, narrow old road. Kind of dangerous with as much traffic as there is these days.''

"Thanks,'' Emily said.

"Give Marty my regards,'' Sally called as Emily closed the door.

Emily went back to the inn to decide what she would do next. She was relieved that the funeral was off, but her plane didn't leave Austin until two tomorrow afternoon. She went into the office and picked up a local map, a few brochures about attractions, and a local newspaper. Back in her room, Emily decided to call Nita and see if she could arrange a visit with her. She found their listing in the thin local phone directory and dialed the number, not knowing quite what she would say. Nita might not even want to see her.

No one answered. Would Nita have gone back to work on the day her husband's funeral was to have taken place? Looking in the phone book under Hays County, she saw the listing for the clerk's office.

"Is Nita Martin in?'' she asked.

"Yes. Just a minute.''

"Hello? This is Nita.''

Emily took a deep breath.

"Mrs. Martin, my name's Emily Stone. I'm a close friend of Marty Rose, and I flew in this morning for the funeral on Marty's behalf. He really wanted to come, but he just couldn't arrange it, and he wanted me to come and convey his sympathy. We're both so sorry to hear of your loss.''

"Thank you,'' Nita said, sounding cautious. "Do you know the funeral's been put off?''

"Yes,'' Emily said. "I learned that after I arrived. I know this must be a difficult time for you, but I was wondering if I might see you. I'd like to meet you, and Marty especially wanted me to visit with you, to tell you how much Chick meant to him. Could we get together later?''

''Yes,'' Nita said. ''I have something that I wanted to give to Marty. I kind of thought he might be here, but I know how busy he must be. I had to come into the office this morning, but I'm going home shortly. Could you come out to the house, maybe around noon?''

''That would be fine.'' Emily wrote down directions to the house, just out of town. When she'd hung up, she wondered how Nita could sound so calm. After Jim had been killed, Emily had taken two weeks off. It had taken that long to pull herself together enough to appear in public. She knew what Nita was going through, but apparently Nita was tougher than Emily had been.

Next, she tried to reach Marty. She had forgotten to find out where he'd be staying in Nashville, so she called Tammy to get the number.

''Did the flowers arrive okay?'' Tammy asked.

''I don't know. The funeral's been postponed,'' Emily said. ''That's why I need to get hold of Marty.''

''I didn't see him this morning,'' Tammy said. ''I'm not sure what time he was planning to leave. His meeting's not until this afternoon. Why'd they postpone the funeral?''

''I don't know for sure. Some kind of inquiry. Where's he staying?''

Emily didn't expect Marty to be in his hotel yet, but she left a message for him to call her when he got in.

Emily changed out of her black dress into cotton slacks and a beige blouse and sat on the bed to read the paper. On the front page of the thin paper was a bold headline: ''Inquest Requested in Teacher's Death.'' The story said that despite initial assumptions that Chick Martin had fallen from his roof and hit his head, the coroner had asked for an inquest. The coroner had declined to comment on the case except to say the body was being sent

to Austin. That was followed by testimonial quotes from
fellow teachers and students, all saying what a wonderful
man Chick Martin had been.

Emily found the Martins house with no trouble. It was
as Sally had said, a neat house with a pretty yard. There
were several other modest homes along the county road,
each with large yards. As she pulled up, Emily could see
a pen of chickens behind the house. A streamer of yellow
police tape fluttered in the breeze along one side of the
house, wrapped from bush to bush around a bed of roses.
As she approached the house, Nita opened the screen
door.

"You must be Emily."

"Yes. It's nice to meet you, Nita." They shook hands,
and Nita held the door open. "I just wish it were under
other circumstances."

"Please, sit down," Nita said, indicating a floral vel-
veteen couch. There was a mildly antiseptic pine scent in
the air. Nita was trim, athletic looking, and wore no
makeup. Her straw-colored hair, showing streaks of gray,
was pulled back with a hair clip. She wore a pale yellow
cotton dress and flat shoes. Emily saw a plain gold band
on her left hand.

"Can I get you something to drink? Iced tea?" Nita
asked.

"Yes, please, if it's not too much trouble."

Nita went into the kitchen, and Emily looked around,
seeing just what she had pictured. Comfortably furnished,
but plain. An arrangement of silk flowers rested on the
dark pine coffee table. A large maple-framed print of a
horse standing in a grove of trees hung on one wall. The
television held an assortment of family photos: the two
boys in baseball jerseys, a graduation picture of each of
them, and a portrait of the four Martins. The all-American
family. It made Emily wistful.

When Nita came back with two glasses of tea, she sat on the couch with Emily.

"I was really hoping Marty would come down," she said. "I can't remember the last time we saw him."

"He was so sorry not to make it, but he had a meeting in Nashville that he just couldn't reschedule. He really felt terrible about it."

"And you came for nothing," Nita said. "I never thought to call anyone about the funeral being postponed. I haven't been thinking too clearly these past few days."

"I understand," Emily said. "I lost my husband suddenly three years ago. You seem to be holding up a lot better than I did. I couldn't even make myself go back to work for awhile."

"I had to," Nita said. "I didn't want to stay around here. Of course, the boys offered to stay home with me, but they've both got summer jobs in Austin, and there wasn't any reason for them to be here. The nights are the worst."

Emily could see tears in Nita's eyes. At first, Nita seemed cautious and distant. After all, she didn't know who Emily was. After a few minutes of strained conversation about the recent hot weather, Nita asked Emily if she'd known Marty for long, and Emily told Nita that they'd been dating for a few months. She confided to Nita that she thought Marty was a wonderful man, and that he'd brought a lot of happiness back into her life.

"Tell me about your lives in Branson," Nita said, warming to Emily. "It must be very exciting."

Emily told her a little bit about Marty's birthday party, but she didn't want to make things sound as lavish as they'd been. Maybe Nita held some resentment toward Marty's success.

Nita put that doubt to rest.

"I know Marty never really wanted to be rich," Nita said. "He just wanted to entertain people. I don't think

Chick had that same kind of drive. But Marty's been so generous to us. Did you know Chick still gets royalty checks from the song they wrote together way back when? Marty could have kept all that because he was the one that got it published and made it into a big hit. But he said, no, that wouldn't be fair. There have been a few times, especially when Chick was going to the teachers' college, that those checks really kept us afloat.''

Emily was touched; Marty had never mentioned this.

''Marty's told me how much Chick meant to him, how he taught him to play guitar and started the Cadillac Cowboys,'' Emily said. ''At the birthday party, he sang a tribute to Chick—'Two Hearts Tied'. ''

''That was the song they wrote together,'' Nita said, the tears welling up again. ''They were real close. We all were. It was really a small town then.'' Nita stood up and went to a desk in the corner. She came back carrying a scrapbook.

''I was going to give this to Marty when I saw him,'' she said, sitting down closer to Emily. ''It's a scrapbook that Chick kept about the Cadillac Cowboys. I think Marty might like to have it.''

She handed it to Emily. The old book smelled a little musty and the yellowed pages were dry with age. Emily opened the scrapbook to the first page where a small newspaper clipping announced the Cadillac Cowboys were to play at the Palamino Lounge on Saturday night.

''This is wonderful,'' Emily said, turning the page. ''I know Marty will really appreciate having this.''

There were lots of snapshots of an adolescent Marty with Nita and Chick, some taken at a picnic on a lake, some with an old Chevy in the background. Emily felt like she was invading private territory. She wished she'd have known Marty then, when he was still a naive kid.

''We've all sure aged, haven't we?'' Nita said with a wan smile.

In paging through the album, Emily saw that photos of the band showed only two Cadillac Cowboys. Some pictures had been trimmed so that only Chick and Marty remained in the shot. In one, she could see someone else's arm at the edge of the shot, resting on Marty's shoulder. But there were no photos including the third player's face.

"Weren't there three of them in the band?" Emily asked, not sure if she should be so nosy.

"Yes, but they had a falling out when the band broke up," Nita said. Her voice was flat and emotionless, but Emily sensed that she knew more than she was saying.

Emily closed the album at the place where a dark red rose was pressed between the pages.

"Marty told me things changed after what happened on Devil's Ridge," Emily said, watching Nita's face.

Nita shot a quick look at Emily, her eyes widening.

"What did he tell you about that?"

"Well, nothing, really," Emily said. "Just that something bad happened there. What is Devil's Ridge?"

Nita got up from the couch and walked to the window looking out on the rose garden.

"Devil's Ridge is just a stretch of highway," Nita said quietly, her back to Emily. She paused. "There's a trail from the road to an old swimming hole on a stream. It's close to Canyon Lake," she said. "The three of us used to go there a lot."

Emily decided to press on. "Nita, I have to ask you. Why is the coroner having an inquest? We thought it was an accident."

When Nita faced her, it was Emily's turn to be shocked. There was an unmistakable look of fear on Nita's face, as though she'd just seen Chick's ghost stand up in the rose bed.

"I don't know what happened," Nita said. "Everyone assumed he'd been up on the roof, but I know Chick wouldn't have done that unless I'd been here. He was always nervous about heights."

"You don't think someone . . ." Emily stopped. She couldn't suggest to Nita that someone might have killed Chick. It was too horrible a thought to voice. But she didn't have to finish the sentence.

"Devil's Ridge killed him," Nita said almost inaudibly. Emily could see her trembling.

"What do you mean?" Emily asked. "What happened out there?"

Nita took a Kleenex out of her pocket and blew her nose. She took a deep breath.

"I can't talk about it," Nita said. "I should never have said those words. Chick wouldn't have, and Marty better not. What happened was a long time ago. Chick and Marty were only sixteen, and they never got in trouble over it. We have to forget about it. I hope we can."

"How could that have something to do with what happened to Chick?" Emily asked. "It was so long ago."

"I'm not sure," Nita said with a sigh. "I just have this awful feeling about it. You shouldn't be asking questions."

"But I'm trying to get close to Marty," Emily said. "I love him, and I really want to know him. I want to know everything about his past. Maybe if you told me about Devil's Ridge I could help Marty deal with it."

Nita looked at Emily, and her eyes narrowed. "I can't tell you what I don't know. Chick tried to put it behind him, but every time he got a royalty check for that song, I could see the past come back to haunt him. I never asked Chick to tell me about it. If you love Marty, you'll never bring it up again."

The visit was clearly winding down. Nita was distant, and Emily realized she didn't want to talk anymore. Finally, Nita said to thank Marty for the beautiful floral arrangement, subtly ending the visit. When Emily left, the scrapbook under her arm, she wanted to hug Nita, to somehow comfort her. But Nita was lost in the past.

Back at the motel, Emily put in another call to Marty's hotel. It was nearly one, and she thought she might still be able to catch him before his meeting at TNN. The desk clerk said he'd checked in but wasn't in his room. Emily left another message.

Emily sat down at the small table in the motel and paged through the scrapbook again, looking for some clue that might help her understand why Marty and Nita were so secretive about the past. When she reached the page that held the rose, she picked it up gently, expecting the petals to be dry and crisp. But the rose was still moist. It gave off a heavy odor, like something just beginning to rot.

☆ CHAPTER 8 ☆

Marty's sleek silver jet landed smoothly in Nashville at noon, and John, who doubled as pilot and chauffeur, opened the plane door for Marty.

They walked through the terminal together, John carrying Marty's bag. Marty kept his sunglasses on, but no one seemed to recognize him. While Marty bought a *Nashville Tennessean* at the gift shop, John got the keys to the rented Cadillac Tammy had reserved for them. A nice plane, nice cars, and a generous salary: John liked his job. He drove Marty to the luxurious Opryland Hotel, pulled up in front, and handed Marty's bag to a smartly uniformed bellhop.

"Why don't you give me one of those keys in case I want to take a drive before the meeting," Marty said to John.

As Marty walked through the lobby, two men wearing suits seated near the reservation desk watched him. One nodded slightly to the other, but neither stood until Marty had his key card and turned to follow the bellhop to his suite. The two men strolled at a discreet distance behind them, stopping at an elevator while the bellhop unlocked the door and took his bag into the room.

As soon as Marty tipped the bellhop and closed the

door, he went into the bedroom, picked up the phone, and dialed a number written on a scrap of paper.

"The Nashville Network," an operator said. "How may I direct your call?"

Marty asked for Bill Johnson and waited. "Bill? Marty Rose. Yes, a good trip. Nice to be here. What time should we get together this afternoon? Three will be fine. I'll see you then. Good-bye."

Marty hung up as a knock sounded on his door. He opened it and looked at the two men standing there.

"Can I help you?" Marty asked.

"Are you Marty Rose?" one man asked.

Caution's red flag waved in front of Marty's eyes.

"Who wants to know?" he asked.

The man who had spoken pulled a leather case out of his breast pocket and flipped it open, revealing a shiny badge.

"We're investigators with the Nashville Police Department. Homicide. We'd like to talk with you briefly if you don't mind," he said.

"What's this all about?" Marty asked, glancing down the deserted hallway.

"You may have heard of the death of your agent Zach Zimrest?" the man said. "We're talking to people who knew him. We could talk to you here, or you could ride with us down to headquarters."

"Well, now, I don't know what kind of a driver you are, so maybe you better just step inside," Marty said with a smile. He opened the door wider. "Have a seat." The two detectives sat side by side on the couch. Marty sat in a chair facing them.

"Were you aware Mr. Zimrest was shot sometime Friday night?"

"Yes. Someone called me yesterday and told me," Marty said. "It's a terrible thing. He'd been my agent and a good friend for years."

"Do you know of any reason someone would want to kill him?" The same detective did all the talking while his partner took notes in a small pocket notebook.

"I can't think of a single reason," Marty insisted. "Zach was a good family man, and he was respected in his field. Why do you think someone killed him?"

The questioner stared at Marty. "Our investigation's just beginning, Mr. Rose. When was the last time you saw Mr. Zimrest?"

Marty leaned back in his chair and pulled at his ear lobe. "Well, I'd have to check back in my calendar for sure, but I think it was about a month ago. Maybe six weeks. I stay pretty busy over in Branson," he said, smiling. "Ever been there?"

"No." Marty looked at the man taking notes.

"Uh, no, I haven't," the other man said.

"We understood that you were in Nashville last week, performing at the state fair?"

"That's right," Marty said.

"Did you see Mr. Zimrest then?"

"No. I had to get right back for a special benefit show," Marty said. "Raised sixty-five thousand dollars for the Women's Crisis Center."

The detective showed no sign of being impressed. "Are you aware that Mr. Zimrest has been under investigation for some time?"

"No," said Marty shocked. "For what?"

"Do you have an accountant, Mr. Rose?"

"Sure. Between the accountant and Zach, they take care of all my business," Marty said.

"Have you heard rumors of any misconduct on Mr. Zimrest's part?"

"No," Marty said. He stood up from the table. "Sounds to me more like you guys are trying to nail Zach rather than find his killer. Is this going to take much longer? I've got an appointment."

The two men stood. "Is there someone that can verify your whereabouts last Friday night?"

Marty glared at them. "Yes."

"Can you tell us how to contact that person?"

"I could, but I'm not going to. Are you trying to implicate me in this thing?"

"No," the detective said coolly. "But we may ask you that question again. Do you have any plans to leave the country?"

"Not that I know of, but if they want me to do a concert in Rio, I'm not going to turn it down."

"We'd prefer that you didn't leave the country until the investigation into Mr. Zimrest's death is closed. How long will you be in Nashville?"

"How'd you guys know I was here anyway?"

"We telephoned your office this morning, and your secretary told us where you were. Was that private information?"

"It's not something she'd tell everyone who calls asking for me," Marty said.

"Well, I guess she thought telling the police was a good idea." A slight smile crossed the detective's lips. "When will you be going back?"

"Tomorrow," Marty said, opening the door. The two men walked out. The detective turned and handed Marty a business card. "Thank you for your help. If you think of any pertinent information, don't hesitate to call. Have a good day."

In the hallway, he turned back to Marty.

"One more thing," the man said. "You wouldn't happen to know why Mr. Zimrest had a rose stuck in his suit pocket when he was found, do you?"

"A rose! Hell, no. A rose?" Marty asked.

The man nodded. "Probably nothing," he said. "Good day, sir."

"Son of a bitch," Marty said under his breath as he

watched them walk toward the elevator. He closed the door, immediately went to the phone and dialed a number from memory.

"Hey, good looking. You got time for an old friend? Great. I'll be there in twenty minutes. I have some things I need to talk over with you. Can't wait to see you. Bye."

Marty drove south on Briley Parkway, getting off at Old Hickory Boulevard. It was ten minutes to one, and he had plenty of time before his meeting. He turned into the Brentwood section, home to Nashville's elite, from city officials to legends of the music industry. The homes here were posh, more lavish than the homes of most stars in Branson, although Marty's could have been transplanted from the lakeside to this neighborhood and fit right in. The well-manicured yards shone like emeralds. The mansions sat well back on each property. Some were surrounded by concrete walls so only a glimpse of tall, white columns could be seen by curious passersby clutching maps to the stars' homes. Other homes were visible through the stately old hickory and magnolia trees that shaded the yards. The neighborhood smelled of freshly mown lawns—and money.

Marty pulled into a long circular driveway and drove past thick foliage that nearly hid the house. It wasn't as lavish as some of the homes, but it could hardly be called modest. As Marty pulled up to the front door, a redhead came out on the porch.

"Darlin', you're looking beautiful." Marty gave her a hug and kissed her on the neck. "Take me inside."

"I didn't know I'd be seeing you again so soon, baby," the woman said. She was tall and slender. Her white satin jogging suit was a stark contrast to her brilliant, flaming mane of hair.

"You want a drink?" She showed Marty into a long living room, dominated by giant tropical plants. Streaks of sunlight filtered through mahogany shutters. They walked noiselessly on the Persian rugs and sat together on a white leather couch.

"Come here and give me another hug," Marty said. "That's what I need."

After holding each other for a moment, the woman pulled away and looked at Marty.

"What's the matter with you, sonny? You look like hell."

"Did you hear about Zach?"

"Yes. Now you want that drink?"

"No, thanks." Marty ran his fingers through his hair and leaned back on the couch. "I've got to be at the network soon, and I sure don't want anything stronger than milk on my breath."

Marty looked at her. "We've been friends a long time, haven't we?"

"A long time," she said. "Let's not think about how long."

"Would you do something for me?"

"What the hell's this about? You know I'd do anything for you except marry you, you big ol' fool."

"What if I needed an alibi, and you were it?"

"Why do you need an alibi?"

Marty got up and went to the grand piano in front of the windows. He picked up a piece of sheet music, idly rolling it into a tube.

"The cops came by my hotel. I hadn't been there ten minutes. They asked me where I was last Friday night."

"Whoa," the redhead said. "No kidding. Did you kill Zach?"

Marty whapped the rolled up music on the piano. "Hell, you know where I was last Friday night. Or have you forgotten?"

"No, but I'd rather not go tell it to the cops," she said.

"Charles might get a little testy about that. Or did you forget I've got a hubby?"

"He knows we're still friends."

"He doesn't know we have sleepovers. Besides, why would the cops suspect you?"

"I don't know," Marty said, sitting down on the piano bench. "I swear to God, I'm not sure I know anything anymore."

The woman took a sip from a tall glass of water with a slice of lemon floating in it. "You didn't tell them you were here, did you?"

"Of course not. But what if it came to that? Would you stick with me on this? Charles would get over it. We could say we just talked all night."

The woman's laugh was throaty and bitter. "Sure, honey. And he'd believe Elvis is alive."

"I'm serious," Marty said. "This is a bad deal, and I want to know who my friends are."

"Where do you get off talking to me that way? You know I'm your friend." She stood up and walked behind the couch.

"Would you do it?"

"Don't press your luck."

"Would you?"

The woman walked slowly over to the piano bench and put her arms around Marty, pressing his head against her full bosom. She stroked his hair, and he could smell the sweetness of her perfume. They were silent for several moments. Then she took him by the shoulders, looking down at him.

"Why don't you ask me that again if it gets to a crunch? How about that? You've got yourself all upset for nothing. This is going to blow over. I promise."

Marty sighed. "You're probably right," he said. "I guess there's just too much going on in my life right now."

"You need to relax." She rubbed his temples. "Charles is out of town again. Why don't you let me work a little of my special magic on you."

Marty stood up and gave her a long kiss. He pulled back and looked at her. "You're something," he said. "I'd love to stay, but I need to be keyed up for this meeting."

She pouted. "Well, call me when it's over and we'll go celebrate."

Marty squeezed her chin. "I'll do that." He strode toward the door, twirling the car keys. "See ya," he called.

At two forty-five, John drove Marty to the offices of The Nashville Network. Three hours later, he walked out with a signed contract in hand and a wide grin on his face. It wasn't as much money as he'd hoped to get up front, but it was enough to pay off most of the money he owed Tommy. He was sure he could get a bank to lend him the rest, based on the piece of paper he held in his hand. The TNN contract was open-ended. They'd televise his bang-up Fourth of July show live from the Crystal Rose Theatre in Branson in ten days. If the ratings were high enough—and Marty was confident they would be—the network would broadcast a Saturday night show live from his theater for sixteen weeks—with an option for more. Tommy Jamison could get stuffed. They could all get stuffed. Nashville was ready for a big bite of Branson, and they'd known who to call.

Marty's smile disappeared when he remembered what he'd learned during the course of the meeting. Now he was certain Zach and Tommy had been working against him. He'd heard about the tapes Zach had said he would deliver and never did. And the TNN brass recounted a lunch meeting with Tommy who had told the executives, very confidentially, that Marty was hitting the bottle and wasn't a good risk. And right on the heels of these bad impressions, Zach goes and gets killed. So Marty had had to do some fast talking. But he'd gone in with videotapes of some of his recent shows, ticket-sale numbers that Tammy had prepared, and the talent lineup for the show on the Fourth. That and a little bit of Marty Rose charm did the trick.

"Well? How'd it go?" John asked as he opened the door for Marty.

"Perfect," Marty said. "They know talent when they see it."

When Marty got back to the hotel, he told John to pick him up at nine.

"We're going to celebrate tonight," he said. "Dress up, slick back your hair, and shine your boots."

"We going anyplace in particular?" John asked.

"We're going to every hot club in town tonight, son," Marty said. "Tonight we play Nashville. In ten days, we play the nation."

★ CHAPTER 9 ★

At five thirty Tuesday afternoon, Tammy was ready to leave the office. She had intended to get out no later than four. With Marty out of town, there should have been less work. Not that she had a lot of other things to do. Her life revolved around handling Marty's needs. She didn't resent that. After all, someone had to take care of him, and she was fiercely protective. Her main job was buffering him from the con artists, the users, and the jerks who so often filled his waiting room. Tammy thought she'd heard it all, more than once.

"He kept looking at me out in the audience, and waving and winking, so I just wanted to meet him. I know he'll be impressed with my singing."

Marty waved and winked at everyone. And when he really needed a backup singer, he called his agent. There was an endless lineup of salesmen pitching everything from new sound equipment to advertising gimmicks to the latest in flashy costumes. Those she sent to Marty's theater manager, marketing director, and costumer. Rarely did anyone get past Tammy.

But tonight Marty was out of her hands, and Tammy was entertaining the idea of heading for the Lone Star Saloon for a few drinks. She always found people there she could hang out with for a few hours. That was the good thing about a small town. The downside was that she knew, and had eliminated as possible catches, most of the single men in town. Thirty-one was a bad age to be single in Branson. Most of the men her own age were already married. Or they were divorced. In that case, it usually didn't take Tammy long to discover why their former wives had kicked them out. There were older men, of course, some who were dedicated to remaining single, which didn't fit in with Tammy's long-range plan of finding a nice husband and having a couple of kids. The biological clock wasn't yet sounding the alarm, but she was beginning to get a little anxious. She'd even tried younger men, but that was too depressing. They had grown up on Motley Crüe and Black Sabbath, and they could repeat the lyrics from rap songs. It made Tammy's skin crawl. She had nearly resigned herself to being single for life, but it wasn't a conclusion that brought her any peace.

"So you'll take care of that tomorrow, right, Lance?" Tammy said into the telephone. "Marty said he wanted the new equipment in by Thursday, and you know how he gets if the sound's not right. Okay, great. Thanks a bunch."

She hung up and stacked up the sheath of paperwork before her. "I'm outta here," she said, reaching under the desk for her purse as a light tap sounded at the door.

"Shit," she said. "Come in."

"Hi. I stopped by to see if Marty's in," said the man as he walked into the office.

He was tall with dark brown wavy hair and a rugged face. Not classically handsome, but striking. Something about the intensity of his pale blue eyes made Tammy stop what she was doing. She caught a scent of spicy aftershave.

"He's out of town. Was he expecting you?"

"Well, not exactly," the man said slowly. His voice was deep and resonant and his accent oozed the charm of the Deep South with no trace of a twang.

"We're old friends, and I ran into him in Nashville a few months back. I told him I'd look him up next time I was in town."

Tammy had heard this one before, but this man exuded such self-assurance that Tammy believed him.

"I'm sorry," the man said. "Forgive my rudeness. My name's Stoney Barnes. And you must be—," he glanced at the name plate on the desk, "—Tammy Farrell." He stepped forward and extended his hand across the desk. "Pleased to make your acquaintance, Miss Tammy."

Tammy extended her hand. This guy had a certain charisma, that was for sure. And he made points by not shaking the hell out of her hand as so many men did. Instead, he held it lightly for a moment, his eyes looking directly into hers.

Tammy withdrew her hand, her normal composure failing her. She fumbled with the snap on her purse.

"Marty won't be back until late tomorrow or possibly Thursday. Will you be staying?"

"I believe I will be in town for some time, and I'd be pleased if you told him I came by. I'll call next week and see what his schedule's like. I know he's a busy man."

"Yes, he is," Tammy said, standing up. "I was just about to leave."

"May I walk out with you?" he asked.

"Sure. Suit yourself."

He opened the door for Tammy, scoring a couple more points for good manners.

"So you live in Nashville?" she asked as they walked down the wide stairs.

"I travel a great deal," he said. "Toronto is my home."

"You don't sound Canadian."

"I'm not," he said. "Raised in Georgia, I'm proud to say."

"Is this your first trip to Branson?"

"Yes. Quite an amazing place, from what I've seen. I'm still trying to find my way around."

"There are maps in the lobby."

He laughed, a soft sound that made Tammy smile. "You're a kind woman. I wonder if you could recommend a good place for dinner?"

"I always recommend Dante's, but it's on the high-priced side," said Tammy.

"How's the food?"

"Wonderful. Real gourmet. Takes about two hours to get through all the courses."

He stopped at the bottom of the stairs and turned to her.

"I apologize for my boldness, but I wondered if you might be so kind as to join me there for dinner tonight?"

There's an idea, Tammy thought. She'd never been to Dante's for dinner because the guys she hung around with knew that a meal for two there could run a hundred bucks or more. Apparently none of them considered her worth that investment.

"I'm sorry. I've offended you," he said.

"Oh, no," Tammy said, smiling. "It's just that I don't know you. You could be some wacko for all I know."

What a stupid thing to say, Tammy thought.

"I understand," Stoney said. "Perhaps another time when we're better acquainted, and hopefully, with Marty's blessing. It's been a pleasure meeting you, Miss Tammy, and I'll look forward to seeing you next week." He turned and strolled toward the front doors.

"Mr. Barnes?" Tammy called. She really didn't want to face another night cruising at the Lone Star. She walked toward him.

"I've reconsidered. I'd be pleased to have dinner with you tonight. I just need to go home and change. We could meet there at say, seven?"

His face lit with a wide smile.

"That would be very kind of you," he said. "I hate eating alone. Can you give me directions?"

Tammy drew a map to Dante's on the back of one of Marty's brochures.

"Thank you," Stoney said. When he reached for the brochure, his fingertips touched her hand, shooting a little thrill up the back of Tammy's neck.

"I'll look forward to seeing you later."

Tammy was walking on air. I've got a date with a guy who might really be cool, she thought. Where's the harm? I'm not driving anywhere with him. We'll be out in public. And if he gets out of line, I'll just leave. And if he gets boring, I'll just eat and leave. She was very pleased with herself although she wished she'd had a chance to ask him what he did for a living. But if he lives in Toronto and travels around, he could have some bucks, she decided.

At seven ten, Tammy pulled up to Dante's. She checked out the cars in front. None had out-of-state plates, so she assumed Stoney was driving a rental. As she walked into the hotel lobby, Stoney stood and came to meet her. Tammy was pleased to see he'd dressed up for the occasion, changing from the tidy jeans and shirt he'd worn to a handsome dark suit and a white shirt with a maroon tie that matched the handkerchief peeking from his breast pocket. Tammy hoped she looked presentable even though the mauve rayon dress she'd chosen was getting a bit snug in the hips.

"I'm happy to see you," he said. "I was afraid you might have thought better of joining me. You look lovely."

A waiter seated them at a white-clothed table. Several

other couples were in the cozy dining room. They all looked well dressed and well heeled, Tammy noted. One elderly couple barely seemed able to lift their forks, their hands were so weighted by glittering rings.

Through the entire evening, Stoney didn't make a mistake. In fact, if Tammy had scripted the scene, he couldn't have been a better escort. First there were cocktails: a Manhattan at her request, a Glenlivit straight up for him. She'd always thought Scotch drinkers were classy. He looked over the menu, then talked with the waiter, asking details of the sauces and the cuts of beef. He suggested Tammy try the Wellington of beef tenderloin if she liked beef. It was the most expensive item on the menu. He suggested they have an appetizer of shrimp and lobster cocktail, and the Caesar salad. The waiter, sensing he was dealing with a gentleman of taste, and sensing a good tip, suggested they try a bottle of Gundlach Bunschu Merlot with dinner.

"That's a good suggestion, but I prefer something a little drier," Stoney said. "Would you happen to have a Chateau Latour?"

It was the best wine Tammy had ever tasted, even at Marty's parties. She didn't know the price, but she was thoroughly impressed. Through the course of the meal, she quizzed him relentlessly, looking for the chink in the armor. But she saw none. Unless the man was a skilled liar, she had found her dreamboat.

He said he was forty, the outer limit of Tammy's preconceived age barrier, but acceptable. Yes, he'd been married, soon after graduating from Georgia Tech, but his wife had been killed in a car accident two years later. They'd had no children. He was a developer of sorts, he told her, putting together investors and dreamers. From that had come a shopping mall in Tampa; a subdivision in Taos, New Mexico; and his latest project, a theme park in Australia. Stoney said he'd begun to think the traveling was too much and that he'd like to settle down. But he hadn't found the right woman. So many these days were abrasive and even got upset if he opened the door for them, part of the courtesy his mother, rest her soul, had taught him, he said. He hoped to find a secure woman, one who shared his interest in reading, in good music, in travel. And he said he hoped it was not too late in his life for children.

"I've died and gone to heaven," Tammy told herself in the restroom while she patted her burgundy lipstick. "*Pleeese* try not to bore this guy."

At ten, they were just finishing bananas Foster. Then there was a glass of fifty-year-old port, good for the digestion, Stoney said. At nearly eleven, Stoney excused himself. It seemed he was gone for a long time, and Tammy wondered if he was indeed a fraud who had run out on the bill. Then he was back, reaching for her hand.

"I would suggest a nightcap elsewhere, but I'm sure you're as tired as I am," he said as he walked her down the street to her car. "I've enjoyed your company, and I hope I may call you again."

"I'd like that." Tammy said. Just take me away with you right now, she thought. "I should have a fairly light day tomorrow. Marty will be back late. If you want to, you could come by, and I'll show you around backstage."

"I'd love it," he said. "Noon? Followed by a long lunch?"

"Great." She watched him in her rearview mirror as she pulled away. She hoped to see what kind of car he was driving, but by the time she turned the corner, he was still walking slowly down the block. Tammy hadn't felt this excited for years.

"This may be too good to be true," she told herself. "But don't be pessimistic. Just wait and see what happens." On the rest of the drive home, Tammy mentally sorted through her closet, planning exactly what she would wear for lunch the next day down to shoes and earrings. For the first time in a long time, Marty Rose never entered her mind.

✶ CHAPTER 10 ✶

Emily woke up Wednesday morning drenched in sweat and scared to death. She'd been dreaming that someone was chasing her. She'd been running for her life. She had taken shelter in an empty grain silo, then realized there was no where to hide. She pulled the covers up around her neck and lay still for a couple minutes, waiting for her subconscious mind to free her from the aftermath of the nightmare. Pursuit dreams were supposed to indicate insecurity. Emily didn't have them often.

While coffee perked in the small coffeemaker in her room, Emily got out her new reading glasses and paged through the scrapbook again, examining every detail. She read all the notices about Cadillac Cowboy appearances. The last one she found was dated in early 1965. Emily thought about trying to call Marty again, but dismissed the idea. He knew where she was.

When she had showered, packed, and checked out, it was ten thirty. Her plane left at two, so she needed to leave Wimberley by noon, and she had one stop she wanted to make before she left.

She parked on the square and walked the half block to the *Wimberley Clarion* office she had noticed yesterday. The weekly newspaper was housed in a small storefront, and a plump older woman wearing thick glasses got up from a desk and came to the counter when Emily walked in.

"May I help you?" the woman drawled.

"I was wondering how far back your archives go?"

"The *Clarion*'s been published since 1955," the woman said with pride. "All our issues before 1987 are on microfilm. Are you doing genealogical research?"

"Yes," Emily lied. "Trying to trace the family tree."

"Have you registered with the Genealogical Society in San Marcos? They have a lot of family names on computer databases there. It can be a lot quicker than searching through our back issues. Saves eye strain," the woman said with a smile.

"No, I didn't know that," Emily said. "I'll call them. While I'm here, I may as well look through some of the issues. I'm interested in 1965."

"Oh, that's not so far back," the woman said, her eyebrows slightly raised. "Was your family living here then?"

"I'm not sure," Emily said. "That's why I wanted to scan the obituaries for that year." She hadn't been prepared with a subterfuge for her search, but suddenly she felt one was needed.

"Come in the back room, and I'll show you how to use the machine," the woman said. "You can make copies for a dime apiece, and I can give you change."

Emily sat at the microfilm reader while the woman went through the details of operating it. From a row of cabinets along one wall, she pulled out a box that held five reels of microfilm, each dated 1965. The woman loaded the first reel and found a page with obituaries.

"It looks like the obits were run on page four in those days, so you can fast forward to those pages through each reel." She stood looking over Emily's shoulder as Emily scanned the death notices for January 5, 1965.

"Thank you," Emily said. "I appreciate your help," hoping the woman would go away.

"If you need anything, I'll be right here," she said, and went back to her desk which was within sight of Emily at the microfilm machine.

Emily began rolling through the pages of the old newspaper. She fast-forwarded until she reached issues in June, the last play date she'd seen in the scrapbook. This is probably a waste of time, she thought, as she passed articles about church socials, wire stories about Vietnam, features about the town's new bank. Maybe Chick just stopped keeping the scrapbook, and she wasn't even looking at the right year. Maybe there hadn't ever been a newspaper story about what happened at Devil's Ridge.

"Doing all right?" the woman called from time to time, peering at Emily through the thick glasses.

After forty minutes, Emily was about to give up. She was already in early September. If Chick and Marty had gone to Devil's Ridge to swim, it wouldn't be much later in the year than that, Emily reasoned.

She was slowly running through the newspaper for the second week in September when she saw the headline: "Woman's Body Found Near Canyon Lake." It was a short notice. It said the partially clothed body of an unidentified woman had been found at the bottom of a bluff along Devil's Ridge, not far from the lake. The body had been found by two local boys. The woman apparently had died from stab wounds. The presumption was that the woman had been killed elsewhere and her body dumped along the remote trail. The Comal County Sheriff's Department was investigating. Emily scanned ahead for the next twelve weeks. There was no other mention of the case, so she returned to the article and put her dime in the copier.

As soon as the machine whirred into action, Miss

Thickglasses bustled on back. "Find something?" she asked.

Emily didn't want the woman to see what she had copied, so as the copy came out a chute on the side of the machine, Emily took a quick glimpse to make sure it had copied, then quickly folded the page in half. "Fine," she told the woman standing behind her. "Came out fine."

As the machine finished its copy mode, the screen light came back on and illuminated the page she had copied. It obviously wasn't the obits.

"This is very interesting reading," Emily said. "There are just a couple of other copies I want to make and then I'll be finished."

"Take your time," the woman said. "I'm glad you're finding what you want. But I'm sure if you call the Genealogical Society, they'll be a lot more help."

"I will," Emily assured. She sat at the machine for another five minutes, and randomly ran copies of two more pages. She wasn't sure why she felt such a need to be so secretive about this. Maybe it was her still lingering feelings of paranoia from this morning's bad dream.

She thanked the woman and left the newspaper with the article tucked in her purse. As soon as Emily closed the door, the woman went to her telephone and dialed a number.

"Wade," she said. "It's me. An odd thing just happened."

Since she still had an hour before she had to leave, Emily decided to get a bite to eat before the drive back to Austin. She was parked near the John Henry Restaurant. She could see through the windows that the place was fairly crowded, but she definitely didn't want to go back to the Cypress Creek Cafe and encounter Sally again. Emily spotted one unoccupied table in the back corner of the restaurant and sat down. It looked like this was where the locals ate because people greeted each other and chatted between tables like it was a PTA meeting.

Emily was eating a turkey club sandwich when she saw a portly man wearing a tan uniform and a white Stetson come in. Several people in the restaurant greeted him. "Hello, Sheriff." The sheriff looked around the restaurant, then walked toward Emily.

"Would you be so kind as to share your table with me?" he said. "It looks like there are no other empty seats."

Emily could see that this was true. "Please," she said, pointing to a chair.

"Thank you," the sheriff said, sitting down with a sigh. He looked like the quintessential Texan lawman, stout and white-haired with deep creases in his tanned face. His walrus moustache was neatly trimmed, and the silver star on his shirtfront was highly polished.

"You're very kind. I'm Sheriff Crockett," he said. "Wade Crockett." He extended a chubby hand across the table.

Emily shook it briefly. "Nice to meet you." She didn't volunteer her name. She didn't want another Sally-type interrogation. She took another bite of her sandwich.

The sheriff ordered a toasted cheese sandwich. When the waitress had gone, he looked at Emily.

"I hear you're a reporter."

Emily stopped chewing her mouthful of food. The sheriff was looking at her steadily and stroking his white mustache. Emily swallowed and cleared her throat.

"No," she said pleasantly. "You've got the wrong person. I'm not a reporter."

"Heard you were looking for something in our newspaper archives? What's your interest in Wimberley?"

Emily was stunned. It sure didn't take long for word to spread in this town. But why would the newspaper clerk have called the sheriff?

The sheriff's steady gaze hadn't wavered.

Emily decided she had to offer some explanation for her presence. The small-town sheriff might get belligerent if she just walked away from him.

"I came for Chick Martin's funeral," Emily said. "I live in Branson, Missouri, and I'm a friend of Marty Rose. He used to be close friends with Chick and his wife, but he was unable to come to the funeral. I found out the funeral's been postponed, and I'll be driving back to Austin to catch my plane this afternoon."

The sheriff leaned back in his chair. Emily heard his leather belt and holster creak. "So you're a friend of Marty's? How's he doing in Branson?"

"Fine," Emily said. She'd eaten only half her sandwich, but now she just wanted to get out of the cafe.

"Still doesn't tell me why you'd be searching the archives of 1965," the sheriff said. The waitress brought his sandwich, but he made no move to eat.

"I was looking up some genealogical information for Marty," Emily said, nervous about lying to the law. "How'd you hear I was at the newspaper?"

"The clerk's my wife. Said you were copying information on Devil's Ridge." The sheriff continued stroking his mustache.

"Why did you think I was a reporter?" Emily asked.

"Just a guess," the sheriff said.

Emily narrowed her eyes and decided to take a chance.

"So what's the big deal about what happened on Devil's Ridge?" she asked. "Nita's scared to death about it. Marty won't talk about it. And now Chick may have been murdered. What's going on, Sheriff?"

"What's your name, ma'am?" the sheriff asked. From the kitchen came the sound of someone dropping a plate.

Emily took a deep breath. Be careful here, girl, she

told herself. She leaned forward and talked slowly and quietly.

"My name's Emily Stone. I used to be a newspaper reporter, but I'm not anymore. I'm Marty's girlfriend. I might be Marty's wife someday. I came down here for a funeral that was canceled because of some inquest. I can't get anyone to tell me what's going on. And if Marty needs protection from some incident in the past, I'm the one that's going to do that."

The sheriff's bushy white eyebrows raised a little.

"Look, Miss Stone," he said. "Your reporter's instinct is off-kilter on this one. There's no mystery here. We've got a standard inquest scheduled for Chick just like anytime someone dies and there's no obvious cause and no witnesses. It's got nothing to do with Marty or anything out of the past."

Emily reached down and took the copy of the newspaper article out of her purse and held it up for the sheriff to see.

"I'll bet you were around here in September 1965," she said. "A woman was stabbed to death by Canyon Lake. . . ."

"Keep your voice down," the sheriff said in a husky whisper, motioning for her to lower the newspaper clipping.

Pay dirt, Emily thought. She slid the clipping back into her purse.

"Look, Sheriff," she said, "I have the best interests at heart of a very public person. If there are some skeletons about to surface here, I think Marty better know about it and be prepared. The next time someone looks up 1965 at the newspaper, it might really be a reporter, and a juicy story in the *Enquirer* could do the hometown boy a lot of damage."

"We're well aware of that," the sheriff said. "We've

been aware of that for thirty years, and we've taken care of it real well.''

"Except now Chick's dead," Emily said.

"That can't have anything to do with the past," the sheriff said. "Just can't." He ate a potato chip.

"You don't sound so sure of that," Emily said. "Who was the woman killed on Devil's Ridge?"

The sheriff ate two more potato chips while he gazed at Emily. He wiped his fingers on a paper napkin.

"A girl from Comal County was killed," he said. "I didn't investigate it, but I was here. I was a deputy. A few days later, the man who killed her was found and convicted. He's still in prison for it. That's all there was to it.''

"What did Chick and Marty have to do with it?"

"Why don't you just leave this alone, and go on home?" the sheriff asked. Emily said nothing.

"Chick and Marty found her body," the sheriff said. He sounded annoyed at Emily's persistence. "They weren't implicated in it in any way.''

"I don't think that's all there is to it," Emily said. "Neither does Nita. Why's she so scared?"

"She has nothing to be afraid of. Cole McCay's locked up behind bars.''

"He was the killer?"

"Yes," the sheriff said. "And justice was done."

"He was in their band, wasn't he?"

"I believe he was, for a time."

"And now it looks like maybe Chick was killed, right?''

"We don't know the cause of Chick's death yet."

"Is Marty in some kind of danger?" Emily had not considered this idea before. She had only thought of the possibility of bad publicity. The idea made the hairs on her arms rise.

"No," the sheriff said firmly. "Absolutely not."

"Tell me the whole story," Emily implored.

"I think that'd be Marty's place to decide what he wants to tell you," the sheriff said. "The best thing is to keep the past in the past."

The sheriff took a bite of the cheese sandwich, and Emily sensed he was saying no more. She fished into her purse for one of her business cards and handed it to him.

"This is my home phone number," she said. "If you find out something that could endanger Marty in any way, please call and tell me. Will you do that, Sheriff?"

"Why wouldn't I just call Marty?"

"It's hard to get hold of Marty," she said. "He's got a lot of people around him that you have to go through, and not all of them are trustworthy. Branson's a small town, too, you know? I'd feel better if you just let me know what's going on, and I'll make sure Marty's the only one who hears about it. In fact, I'll have Marty call you. How's that?"

The sheriff stared at her for a long moment. "I'm not sure why I feel like trusting you except you seem like a straight shooter," he said. "You seem like the kind of woman Marty would hook up with. And I'm glad he's got someone watching out for him—not that he needs it in this regard," the sheriff added quickly.

"All I'm asking is that if something comes up, you'll let me know. Will you do that?"

"I'll hang onto your card, but I'm sure there's nothing that's going to come up."

Emily glanced at her watch. It was nearly noon. "I've got to get to Austin," she said. "My plane leaves at two." Emily stood up and reached into her purse for her wallet. "Let me take care of that," said the sheriff, standing. "I spoiled your lunch. The least I can do is pay for it."

Emily looked at him. It was the first time she'd seen him smile. "Thank you," she said, and extended her hand. "It turned out to be nice meeting you."

"Likewise," the old sheriff replied. "Marty was always a favorite of mine. Tell him Crockett said howdy."

"I'll do that," Emily said. "Don't forget to call me."

"I won't have any reason to call you," the sheriff said.

Emily got in her car and headed toward Austin. She was relieved to be leaving Wimberley. Maybe it was just as well no one had been willing to tell her the whole story. Sometimes ignorance was bliss.

After she left, Wade Crockett ate a few more bites of his cold cheese sandwich. A couple of people stopped by the table to chat, but Crockett seemed lost in thought. When he had settled the bill, he walked back to his small office around the corner from the square. He looked up a number in a directory and dialed. Behind him was an empty jail cell, ready for some drunk to occupy it on Saturday night. That was about the extent of crime in Wimberley.

"Warden? Sheriff Wade Crockett in Wimberley. I wanted to check on the status on one of your prisoners. That's right. A Cole McCay." He spelled the last name. "Sent up in 1965."

The sheriff drummed his fingers on the tidy desk while he waited. "Are you certain? When? All right. Thank you." The sheriff slowly hung up the phone and sat motionless for a full minute, staring into space. "Jesus Christ," he said under his breath.

⋆ CHAPTER 11 ⋆

Anna and Gordon were playing pinochle at the kitchen table when Emily got home from the airport Wednesday night. Each had a mug of beer, and there was a half-empty bowl of salted nuts on the table.

"Little party?" Emily said, setting her suitcase in the hallway.

Anna got up and gave her a hug. Rocko came up and rubbed her legs, berating her loudly for her absence.

"How was the trip?" Anna asked, picking up her hand of cards again. Emily joined them at the table and gave a brief account of the trip. She glossed over the reasons for the funeral's postponement, partly because she was tired, and partly because she didn't want to get into any sensitive subjects in front of Gordon. She wasn't even sure yet how much she would tell Anna.

"How's everything here?" Emily asked.

"Oh, fine," Anna said. "But you'd better start locking your car. There's been a rash of break-ins the last few days around here. Even some poor old man got mugged in a restaurant last night."

"No kidding," Emily said, with little interest. "Any messages for me?"

"I left a few notes on your desk," Anna said, popping

a handful of nuts in her mouth. "Oh, and Marty called about an hour ago. Said to phone him at his office when you get in."

Emily met this news with mixed feelings. She carried her suitcase upstairs and laid it on her bed. When she unlatched the case, a slightly rank smell wafted up from the scrapbook inside. She opened the scrapbook to where the rose was pressed. An ugly spot of green mold showed in its center. Emily delicately picked up the rose by the short piece of stem. She turned toward the wastebasket, then changed her mind and went to her office where she got a small manilla envelope from her desk. She dropped the rose into the envelope, but didn't seal it. She laid the envelope on a book shelf. Then she sat down at the desk and dialed Marty's office.

Marty sounded like he was in a good mood, but he wouldn't tell her how things went in Nashville until he saw her, he said. He'd pick her up in an hour. As she was taking a shower, Emily realized she doubted that Marty would show up as planned. Her faith in him was eroding around the edges like rust creeping over a fender.

When Marty left his office on the way to Emily's, he carried a large envelope, and he was smiling. A few minutes later, he pulled up in front of Tommy Jamison's house and strode up to the front door where he punched the doorbell several times in rapid succession.

Tommy opened the door. He was wearing a sleeveless undershirt and a baggy pair of chinos. His feet were bare and there was a day's stubble on his chin. He certainly didn't look the part of the dashing financier.

"Hey, Marty," Tommy said. His smile showed yellowed teeth. "You made it back! Come on in." He swung open the door. "How'd it go?"

"Was there any doubt that I'd make it back?" Marty asked.

"What do you mean?" Tommy asked. "Come on in here."

"I don't want to come in," Marty said. He held out the envelope.

"What's this?" Tommy said, a note of suspicion sounding in his voice.

"Open it," Marty said.

"What the hell's the matter with you, Marty?" Tommy asked, peering at him in the dim light that filtered out of the hallway. "Come in and tell your old partner what happened in Nashville."

"You're not my partner," Marty said. "Open it."

Tommy opened the envelope and pulled out a sheath of papers. Attached to the top by a paper clip was a check for two hundred and fifty thousand dollars.

Tommy's mouth sagged open slightly when he saw the check. "What kind of joke is this?" He grinned at Marty.

"It's called the last laugh, pal," Marty watched Tommy closely, his hands at his sides, fingers twitching slightly.

"I don't understand," Tommy said, the smile leaving his face.

"It's like this," Marty said. "There's the money I owed you. There's the note I signed to you. There's the line that says paid in full." Marty reached into the inside pocket of his suede jacket. "And here's a pen."

"What kind of horse shit is this?" Tommy whacked the check with the back of his hand. "Where'd you get this kind of money? You passing me a rubber check?" He laughed harshly.

"I got the deal," Marty said. "And you're gone."

Tommy looked confused. "You got the deal?"

"Marty Rose got the deal," Marty said.

"No," Tommy said, "you don't just get a deal like this. You're pulling something here." He started to turn into the house.

Marty had his big hand around Tommy's throat before Tommy could blink. He grabbed the paper out of Tommy's hand, and slammed Tommy up against the open door. The door hit the wall with a loud bang.

"How did a rose get in Zach's pocket when he died, you son of a bitch?" Marty growled, his face inches from Tommy's.

"I don't know what you're talking about," Tommy gasped. He was on his tiptoes, his fingers clutching Marty's wrist.

"Did you kill him, or did you hire someone to do it?" Marty asked, increasing the pressure until Tommy's face was red and contorted with the effort to breathe.

"I didn't do it," he gasped. "Didn't do it."

Marty released his grip on Tommy's neck and grabbed Tommy by the arm. Marty flung him violently toward a table in the hallway. Tommy caught himself, rocking the table. A crystal vase holding silk flowers shattered on the floor.

Marty slapped the papers on the table, slammed down the pen, and said, "Sign it." When Tommy hesitated, Marty grabbed his flabby arm and squeezed it like a vice.

"Okay, okay," Tommy said. He picked up the pen. "You don't want to do this, Marty. We can have a real sweet thing here. You just wait and see what ol' Tommy's putting together."

Marty grabbed the back of Tommy's neck viciously. "Sign it."

When Marty saw that Tommy's signature was shaky but legible, he let go of the man and picked up the paper. He left the check on the table. Tommy was glaring at him and rubbing his throat.

"You'll be sorry," he said shrilly as Marty stepped toward the door. "You're a has-been, and TNN's about to find that out."

In one smooth motion, Marty turned and landed a right

hook on Tommy's jaw. Tommy fell hard to the floor. Marty took a step forward and stood over him. Tommy's eyes were wide with fear. Marty pointed at him and spoke quietly. "Don't you ever show your face around my theater again. And if you ever go near Emily or Anna Stone again, I'll kill you. You understand me?"

Tommy nodded slightly. He made no move to get up.

As Marty pulled out of the driveway, he was rubbing the knuckles of his right hand. He was wincing, but smiling from ear to ear. "Yee-haw," he shouted.

Right on time, Marty pulled up to Emily's. She was glad to see he hadn't come in the limo. Marty wanted to have her all to himself, he said, so they drove out to Moonshine Beach and parked by the lakeshore. It was a beautiful summer night. Despite the pink glow on the horizon from the neon lights of the theater strip, there were twinkling reflections of stars on the dark, calm surface of Table Rock Lake.

With the enthusiasm of a kid who's just scored a home run, Marty told Emily about his success at TNN. Emily felt like a load of bricks had been lifted from her chest. She hadn't realized until that moment just how worried she had been. She would have hated to see Marty's career and reputation ruined. Even if he turned out not to be the love of her life, he meant a lot to many fans, and to the community. She certainly wouldn't wish harm on someone just because he was self-absorbed.

"When I got back this afternoon, I went to the bank," Marty continued. "They loaned me the rest of the money without a hitch because of the contract I'd gotten. And I had them make out a check for the amount I owed Tommy. You should have seen his face!" Marty laughed loudly. "That old boy was hopping mad that his plans went up in smoke." Then his smile disappeared and he fell silent.

"I punched him out too," Marty said quietly.

"You punched him?" Emily asked incredulously.

"Right in the chops," Marty said. Then he couldn't hold back the laughter.

"That's terrible," she said, suppressing a giggle as she pictured the scene.

"And I told him to stay away from you and Anna, too," Marty said. "I hope Anna wasn't too stuck on him. She can do a lot better. I know a nice retired doctor over in Kimberling. I'll introduce them."

"I don't think she'll mind," Emily said, wondering how she would explain to Anna. "So Tommy's not a threat anymore?"

"I'm not so sure," Marty said. "Let's go sit down on the bank." For a few minutes, they sat enjoying the silence. Not even the sound of a boat marred the peace. Marty tossed stones into the lake.

"So talk," Emily said. "Am I going to have to pry it out of you every time?"

"No, no, woman, don't nag at me," Marty said with mock annoyance. "I just don't want to scare you."

"Scare me?"

"I'm afraid Tommy might be behind Zach's murder."

Marty recounted his conversation with the Nashville police, omitting the exchange about his Friday night alibi.

"They found a rosebud in Zach's pocket," Marty said. "I think Tommy might have killed him or else had him killed because some deal they had went sour. Then he thought maybe he could implicate me by leaving the rose. Maybe he thought it was a way to mar my reputation with bad publicity so that TNN would get cold feet about signing with me."

Marty told her what the TNN executives had said about Tommy's ruthless rumormongering. Emily vowed to sit down with Anna and tell her everything. Emily couldn't picture Tommy pumping bullets into anyone, but Anna at least had to hear about the back-stabbing he'd done to Marty.

Marty put his arms around Emily and pulled her down beside him on the sand. It felt good to be with him again, and Emily realized she had missed him.

"Why didn't you call me last night?" she asked.

"I figured you'd already be asleep by the time I got in," he said. "I did a little celebrating. Me and John went to every old juke joint in Nashville, and guess what? A lot of people haven't forgotten ol' Marty Rose. I thought about you a lot. I wish you had been there with me."

They lay together on the sandy shore for a few minutes, listening to the soft lap of the waves on the beach.

"Do you want to hear about my trip?" Emily finally asked.

Marty sat up cross-legged and threw another stone in the water.

"No," he said quietly. "I don't really want to hear about it, but I suppose I have to. How are Nita and the boys?"

"Nita's doing okay," Emily said. "I didn't see the boys."

"They weren't at the funeral?" Marty sounded shocked.

"There wasn't a funeral," Emily said.

In the pale light, Emily could see worry spread on Marty's face as she recounted the entire story up to her conversation with the sheriff.

"What's Nita afraid of?" she asked.

Marty stood up and walked to the water's edge. "I don't know," he said, his back to Emily. "There's nothing to be afraid of."

Emily thought carefully about what to say next. She could keep quiet, but that meant a permanent wall of doubt and suspicion and lies between her and Marty. She knew that ultimately she would leave him if that was the way it had to be.

"Who was the woman Cole McCay killed?"

Marty spun to look at her. "What did you say?"

Emily repeated her question. With his back to the horizon, Marty's face was in shadow.

"You been doing a little investigative work there, darlin'?" Marty asked.

Emily felt the coldness in his voice, and her chest muscled involuntarily tightened. She had to clear her throat before she could speak.

"I just thought that if there's some danger to you, you should be aware of it," Emily said. "Two of your best friends were killed last week."

"This would make a good story for the tabloids, wouldn't it?" Marty asked.

"How you can imply that?" Emily asked, standing up. She stuck her hands in the pockets of her pants. "That's a rotten thing to say."

"Well, what am I supposed to think? You just won't lay off the past," Marty said.

There was silence between them for several moments.

"What if there is some connection?" Emily asked.

"There isn't," Marty said, impatience rising in his voice. "They don't know that Chick was murdered. And even if he was, there's nothing that connects him to Zach. You've got a fine imagination. You ought to write a murder mystery. Just don't write it about me." Marty walked past her toward the car. "You coming?" he asked.

Standing alone on the lakeshore, Emily felt ashamed of herself. He was right. She was manufacturing demons just because she wanted Marty to share his secrets with her, and she wasn't sure how much of her motivation came from a desire to protect him and how much sprung from insecurity. After all, knowledge can be power. She turned and walked to the car. He started the engine as soon as she had closed her door. They rode in silence back to the main highway.

"Look," she began. "You're right. I've gone overboard on this. It's certainly none of my business, and I apologize. Maybe it is an overactive imagination."

Marty didn't say anything.

"You know I'd never do anything to hurt you, don't you?" Emily asked.

He reached out and patted her knee and rested his hand there. She slipped her hand into his.

"I know that, baby," he said. "Here's how things are: I've got a major stumbling block named Tommy out of my way. I've got the show of my life to think about for the next week. I've got my lady by my side, and I feel like I can breathe again. Have you ever felt that way?"

"Absolutely," Emily said. "I'm starting to feel that way now."

"Good," Marty said. "Let's go get a cup of coffee. Then I'm going to take you home. I'm dead tired, and I've got a hell of a week ahead."

Her house was dark when they got home forty minutes later, and Emily was relieved that she didn't have to face Anna. She was bone tired and looking forward to collapsing into bed. She didn't turn on the light. She slid the suitcase onto the floor, shed her clothes, and rolled into bed. She was asleep within two minutes. Sometime after three, Emily woke with a start and sat up. The dream was not the same as the night before. It was worse, and Emily remembered it vividly. The man who had been pursuing her had caught her. They were in the silo, and he was stabbing her over and over. She could see the glint of the knife as it came toward her, tearing her flesh again and again. She couldn't see his face. Emily reached to the nightstand and switched on the light, glancing around the room fearfully even though she knew she was awake and safe. But her ribs hurt, right where the killer had been stabbing her. She looked down and was shocked to see an ugly red mark on her side. What the hell is this? She was trembling a little. Then she saw the scrapbook. It had been on the bed when she went to sleep, and apparently she had rolled over on it, the sharp corner poking into her ribs. The pain of it must have instigated the dream. Emily got out of bed and picked up the scrapbook. She carried it downstairs, flipping through it one last time while the words of Marty, Nita, and the sheriff echoed through her mind. "Leave the past alone." That's exactly what she would do. Tomorrow, Marty's past would be his. His alone.

☆ CHAPTER 12 ☆

Emily didn't think about the scrapbook the next day. Thursday passed quickly as days did when Emily was engrossed in her writing. In the morning she'd gotten a call from an editor at *Traveler* magazine wanting her to do a piece on Branson for their next issue, and Emily started gathering the information she'd need for the article right away. Just before noon, *Country Weekly* called and she agreed to cover an upcoming concert by George Jones in Branson. Emily was pleased that the calls were rolling in.

She had been worried when she first left her newspaper job that she wouldn't be able to make a living as a freelance writer. She had the life insurance money; Jim, always well organized and planning ahead, had left a substantial policy in her name. But she knew that would run out if she didn't find work. It was slow for the first few months, but more and more, editors at a variety of magazines and newspapers had learned that Emily was reliable and competent at producing articles. Branson was often the subject, but not exclusively. One of her favorites had been an article for a national wildlife magazine on some of the remaining natural habitats in Missouri. She'd taken an enjoyable three-day drive for that one, and saw a lot of beautiful country. In the fall, she had a trip booked to Maine, where she'd write about the bed-and-breakfast boom in that state. Her career was right on track. And maybe she'd give some thought to Marty's idea of writing a murder mystery.

For the *Traveler* article, Emily needed to research the history of Branson as it grew into an established vacation destination. She remembered the box of old local magazines Anna had dragged home from an auction a few months earlier. Anna told her the box was still in the corner of her bedroom, so Emily carried it upstairs to her office, where she sat on the floor and sorted through it. It held dozens of back issues of the *Ozark Mountaineer* and *Branson Life* magazines dating back more than a decade. Emily found them fascinating. She got caught up in reading articles about each new entertainer who came to town and built a theater. In the September 1985 issue she found the story announcing groundbreaking for the Crystal Rose Theatre. "Country's favorite balladeer will bring his dream theater to life next spring," the headline read. There was a photograph of Marty wearing a hard hat and holding a shovel. Beside him, a tall, redheaded woman also stood poised with shovel in hand. Emily read the caption. "Marty Rose and his fiancée, singer Patsy O'Rouke, are ready to get started on their next venture."

Emily stared at the picture. She got up and found her reading glasses and looked again. Miss O'Rouke was very pretty. The fiancée Marty had never mentioned to her. Of course Emily knew there must have been a lot of women in his life. A handsome and famous entertainer could have his pick. But seeing Marty with his fiancée made Emily's stomach churn. She tossed the magazine back into the box and carried it out to the garage, setting it with a pile of other boxes she had yet to unpack. When she went back in the house, she brewed herself a strong cup of tea. She sipped it and thought about her trip to

Maine. Maybe she'd invite Anna to go with her. Gradually, the sour taste in her mouth diminished.

On Friday morning, Emily awoke to the sound of something crashing downstairs. She pulled on her robe and rushed to see what had happened.

Anna was pulling things out of the front hall coat closet. Assorted boxes, books, clothes, a broom, and Emily's tennis racket were jumbled in a pile on the floor. Emily could see Anna's rump sticking out of the closet.

"What are you doing?" she asked.

Anna stood up, puffing. "I'm looking for my garage-sale bag," she said. "I could have sworn I put it in here."

"What's a garage-sale bag?" Emily asked. "You'd better put all that stuff back in there. I'm not going to pick it up."

"I will," Anna said. "My net bag. You've seen it. That green bag I always take to garage sales because it holds so much?"

"I don't know," Emily said. She headed for the kitchen, feeling annoyed and groggy. "Are you going to a garage sale?"

"All of them," Anna called.

In the kitchen, Emily took a coffee cup out of a cupboard that had no door. None of the cabinets had doors. Gordon had set about refinishing the doors more than three weeks ago and there seemed to be no sign that the job would ever be finished. An assortment of tools lay scattered on the counter where Gordon had left them.

"Here it is!" Anna called. "Tammy's coming over in a few minutes, and we're going to make the rounds."

Anna was a dedicated garage-sale devotee. It had been hell getting her to weed through the odd and extensive assortment of junk she'd collected over twenty years before they moved to Branson. But Emily had been very firm about a lot of things, insisting Anna have a garage sale of her own. It had been amusing watching Anna in her driveway, bargaining for twenty minutes over the selling price of a crock pot that Anna herself had bought at a garage sale for three dollars.

"Tammy's coming over?" This was a surprise. She hadn't realized that Anna and Tammy were pals. But her mother never ceased to amaze her. Everyone liked Anna. Emily had just sat down with the coffee when the doorbell rang.

"I'll get it," her mother hollered.

Emily heard Tammy's voice, and walked into the living room carrying her coffee. "Hi, Tammy."

"Hi," Tammy said with a smile, looking up from the coffee table where they had spread out a map of Branson. Anna was holding a copy of the newspaper with numerous notices of garage sales circled. Tammy held a notepad and was jotting down locations. Emily watched the two serious plotters. Finally, Tammy folded up the map. Beneath it lay the scrapbook.

"Is this a scrapbook?" Tammy asked, opening the cover. Emily thought for a moment of grabbing it away from her, of running to hide it, but realized how awkward that would look. Besides, there was nothing in there that anyone would find sinister. For the next several minutes, Tammy and Anna paged through the scrapbook, giggling over how young Marty had been.

"Look at those sideburns," Tammy cried gleefully. "Boy, am I going to tease him about this."

Got to tell Marty about the scrapbook today, Emily thought.

"What's Marty doing today?" she asked.

"Same old thing," Tammy said. "Cussing at the guys backstage. I never saw him so wound up. He's driving everyone crazy."

"How come you've got the day off?"

"Because I know he won't be in the office all day,"

Tammy said. "He'll be backstage. So I just put the answering machine on. Also, I've got an appointment to get my hair cut this afternoon." She grinned at the two women. "Because I've got a date tonight."

"No kidding," Anna said. "You sound pretty excited about it."

"I am," Tammy said, picking at a chipped fingernail. "And I'm getting sculptured nails," she said lifting her nose into the air.

"Oooo," Emily said, sounding impressed. "Who's the new Romeo?"

"He's wonderful," Tammy said, a dreamy look in her eyes. "I can't tell you how perfect he is." Tammy listed off all the great traits she'd discovered about Stoney plus an elaborate physical description and details of what he'd worn and what they'd had to eat Tuesday night and at lunch with him Wednesday after she gave him the grand tour of the theater. She barely stopped for breath.

"Sounds like he's too good to be true," Anna said.

"I know. I can barely believe it myself. He'll probably turn out to be a toad tonight." Her face fell.

"Maybe not," Emily said, hoping to reinflate Tammy's enthusiasm. "Where'd you meet him?"

"He stopped by to see Marty while you-all were gone Tuesday," Tammy said. "He's an old friend of Marty's."

"Is he an entertainer?" Emily asked.

"No. He's a financier," Tammy said, careful to pronounce the word correctly. "He said he's written a couple of songs, but nothing that's been published. I don't know exactly how he knows Marty. He built a shopping center in Tampa."

"Oh, really?" Emily said. "Which one?"

"I don't know. I'll ask him tonight. We're going to dinner at the Brass Rail. Tuesday I had Beef Wellington. I think tonight I'll have lobster."

"Does he like his girlfriends plump?" Emily asked without thinking.

Tammy shot her a look of disgust.

"What's his name?" Emily asked, hoping to cover her awkward comment.

"Stoney Barnes," she said. "He lives in Toronto."

"We'd better get going," Anna said, cutting off Tammy's next barrage of description. "All the good stuff will be gone."

"That's a serious concern," Emily teased, earning a quick glare from Anna.

"I'll repack that closet when I get back," she said.

"Good," Emily said. "I want to have a talk with you later too." She had resolved to explain the Marty and Tommy situation before Anna's feelings got hurt when Tommy failed to call anymore.

"My, that sounds serious," Anna said, collecting the map and newspaper and her garage-sale bag. "Am I in trouble?"

They were out the door before Emily could answer.

The *Traveler* article was coming along nicely. Emily thought she would finish it today. She decided against going to the theater to see Marty. Even if she told him about the album, he'd probably be too distracted to listen to her. And there was no reason to go up there and run the risk of getting snubbed. She'd save the scrapbook until things calmed down after the Fourth of July.

By three, the shoppers were back, and Tammy had to hurry off to her hair appointment.

Emily reached the stair landing just in time to see Anna wrestling a beat-up wooden armchair through the front door.

"Look what I got!" Anna crowed. She went out the front door and returned with her bag chock full. Emily could see clothing and books and something that was either a tablecloth or a dress. Anna had had a wonderful time. She was a little mad at Tammy for buying an antique framed mirror "right out of my hands," but Tammy had explained how much she needed it to brighten up a corner of her meager home, so Anna had forgiven her.

Show-and-tell took forty minutes. She'd even bought a couple of blouses for Emily. One was kind of pretty. The other, a loud Hawaiian print, Emily vowed to save in case someone had a luau or a Halloween party. As Emily watched Anna unpacking her treasures, she had to smile. At least her mother was healthy and happy, and that's really all that mattered. Emily hoped Anna wouldn't be too unhappy over losing Tommy. Finally, the time had come.

"Mom, I've got to tell you something, and I don't think you're going to like it too much."

"Are you pregnant?" Anna asked.

"Be serious," Emily said. "Sit down and listen."

Anna sat on the couch and paged through the 1949 cookbook she'd bought. "I'm listening," she said.

Emily began by explaining Tommy and Marty's former business relationship. Then she told what Tommy had tried to do to Marty in Nashville. She even told Anna that Marty suspected Tommy might have been the one who killed Zach. Throughout Emily's monologue, Anna seemed attentive.

"Now here comes the hard part, Mom," Emily said.

She told her about the fight, and about Marty threatening Tommy if he ever came around she or Anna again. When she was through, she watched Anna expectantly.

"Well," Anna said, beginning to refold the pile of garage-sale clothing, "I guess Tommy isn't too worried about Marty because he called me last night, and we've got a date tomorrow. We're going to Springfield to the ballet."

"Mom, you can't do that!" Emily exclaimed. "You

can't go out with him anymore. Didn't you hear a word I just said?"

"Yes, I did," Anna said slowly. "But I've heard it all before."

"What do you mean?"

"Tommy told me all about everything last night," Anna said, standing up to hold a rumpled dress against her chest. "He was pretty upset with Marty at first, but he knows that Marty can be a hothead, as he called it. He'll cool down and they'll be buddies again, Tommy says. You don't see him pressing assault charges against Marty, do you?"

"How can you believe him? What about him threatening to foreclose on Marty?"

"Well, he only did that because he wanted to motivate Marty to work hard on getting the TNN deal. He wanted his money back too. He's looking at a thousand acres out west of Branson where he's going to build a retirement community. Those are the pictures he was showing me after the party."

Emily couldn't believe her ears. Her mother must be the most gullible person in the world.

"That's really an ugly dress," Emily said. "How much did you pay for that?"

"Fifty cents," Anna said. "I know it's kind of dark, but I can wear it around the house for cooking and cleaning."

"I don't know if I can let you go out with Tommy tomorrow," Emily said.

"*Let* me?" Anna looked at her, ready to laugh. "Did we forget who's the mother here?"

"He might have killed Zach. Didn't you hear me?"

"I heard you," Anna said. "Tommy's not a killer. I could tell if something like that were wrong with him. It seems to me that your boyfriend's the violent one. Tommy says his jaw is still swollen."

"All right," Emily said, standing up. "I'm not going to talk about this anymore. You just go ahead and do what you want. But if I were you, I'd take a can of mace with me Saturday night." Emily walked toward the stairs.

Anna rummaged in the bottom of the mesh bag and held up a plastic package. "Brand new, never opened," she said. "One dollar." Emily looked back.

"Pepper spray," Anna said, grinning like a Cheshire cat.

Stoney called Tammy just before he was due to pick her up, apologizing profusely. His rental car had overheated and he'd had to have it towed to a garage. Worse, the car agency was out of cars, so he wouldn't have a vehicle until tomorrow. Tammy's smile disappeared. She had known something was bound to go wrong. She held the telephone a slight distance away from her ear so as not to crush her new bouffant hairdo.

"I could come pick you up," she suggested, with little optimism.

"I have a better idea, if you wouldn't mind," Stoney said, his voice purring through the receiver. "I'm staying at the Lakeshore Inn and that's just a stone's throw from the Brass Rail. I'll walk down and meet you there. I know it's very tacky of me not to be able to pick you up. I could hire a taxi."

"Oh, that's not necessary at all," Tammy said, beaming again. "I won't mind driving over. If I leave now we won't even be late for our reservations. Why don't you let me pick you up?"

"I can walk to the Brass Rail before you can drive to the Inn," Stoney said. "I'll see you there soon, and Tammy?"

"Yes?"

"I'm really looking forward to seeing you."

Tammy closed the bathroom door and looked in the

full-length mirror. The black sheath Anna had found at the last garage sale fit her perfectly. And it had only taken two minutes to sew up the tiny tear under the arm. She loved her hairdo. The ceramic fingernails felt funny but looked great with the pale pink polish the manicurist had suggested. And luckiest of all, in the box of makeup she'd found at the third garage sale was a tube of pink lipstick that just matched her nails.

"You're hot, girl," she jubilantly told her reflection. Driving over to the Brass Rail, Tammy fantasized about after-dinner possibilities. Of course she'd drive Stoney back to the Lakeside Inn. He'd invite her in, put on soft music, and dance slowly with her until he finally picked her up and carried into the bedroom where he would oh-so-gently lay her on the bed. . . . Tammy screeched to a stop at a red light, surpassing the intersection line by a foot. A driver waiting to turn left blasted his horn at her.

Stoney was every bit the perfect gentleman once again. He was wearing the same suit, but Tammy assumed that he probably hadn't brought more than one because he knew that Branson was a casual resort town. He hadn't counted on meeting me, Tammy thought with pleasure. He ordered champagne this time instead of wine, which Tammy thought was a good sign that he was falling for her. Tammy didn't talk about her garage-sale venture. She was afraid he'd find that boring. But she told him all about the old scrapbook of Marty's. She was sure he'd be interested, and he was. Stoney said he'd gotten to know Marty after his Cadillac Cowboy days, but Marty had told him all about those times one night when they were having dinner.

"He seemed very nostalgic for those times," Stoney said. "Sometimes when you look back, the past seems like it was a simple, uncomplicated time. I imagine Marty yearns for that at a time like this. There must be so much pressure on him, getting ready for this huge show. I'm not even going to try to get together with him until that's over. Then he'll need an evening out with an old friend. Maybe you'd be kind enough to join us?''

The idea of double-dating with Marty stunned Tammy. Never before had she had a boyfriend whom she thought enough of to even suggest such a thing.

"Before I forget," Tammy said, opening her satin evening bag, "I brought you this." Proudly she held out a laminated tag on a chain. "All Access Pass," it read. "Fourth of July 1995."

"This way you can just come on backstage, and no one will hassle you. We give out very few of these," Tammy added in a confidential tone.

"You're too much," Stoney said. "What a stroke of luck it was to meet you."

Tammy glowed like a neon marquee. When they ordered dinner, Stoney suggested she have the lobster, but Tammy declined and opted for grilled salmon. She turned down dessert, too, mainly because she didn't want this dinner to drag on all night. What she wanted to do was get Stoney back to the Lakeside Inn.

At first, he declined her offer of a ride, saying it would do him good to walk off his dinner. But Tammy was insistent. Tammy parked in front of the inn lobby, making sure she wasn't in a loading space. When she shut off the motor, Stoney leaned over toward her and turned her face to him. He gave her a lingering kiss. One long one followed by three soft pecks. His lips drifted down her chin. She was paralyzed with pleasure.

"Good night, my dear," he said, opening the car door.

"Wait!" Tammy broke out of the trance. "Could I . . ." Stop, she told herself. Don't scare him off. "I thought maybe we could have a nightcap before I go home."

Stoney sat back down in the car, his right leg still out the open door.

"It's very tempting," he said softly. "But I'm old-fashioned at heart. If I take you in there with me, I'm not sure I could let you leave, and that wouldn't be right. You'd feel that I had taken advantage of you. I would love to, but I want you to know I'm a man of self-restraint."

He put his fingers to his lips and then touched the tip of her nose. "Good night, Miss Tammy. Sweet dreams."

He looked back and waved at her before he opened the door to the inn's lobby.

Damn, Tammy thought, as she pulled out of the parking lot. Damn, damn, damn. Now he probably thinks I'm too fast. She slapped the dashboard. One of the ceramic fingernails snapped and ricochetted off the windshield.

Stoney stood in the doorway and watched Tammy's car pull away. His right hand was in his jacket pocket, fingering the backstage pass. When her taillights were out of sight, Stoney closed the door and walked at a brisk pace in the direction of downtown Branson. He sang softly. *"Angels fly with two hearts tied. . . ."*

☆ CHAPTER 13 ☆

When the wall phone in Emily's kitchen rang Saturday morning, Rocko took a flying leap onto the countertop. He always ran to a ringing telephone, yowling loudly. Emily thought it was because the ringing hurt his ears. Anna thought he did it just to be annoying.

"Get down," Anna shouted at the Siamese, and waved the spatula she was holding. As she answered the phone, Rocko retreated, knocking over the jar of vitamin C that Anna had just uncapped. The pills scattered across the linoleum.

"Damn," Anna said, the phone halfway to her ear. "Hello?" she demanded. Then her tone changed.

"Marty. Hi. No, just the normal morning chaos around here. Emily's not up yet. Do you want me to get her? Okay. I'll tell her as soon as she wakes up. Bye."

Anna hung up and turned back to the stove where two eggs sizzled in a sea of butter in the frying pan. Anna flipped the eggs and reached into a cupboard that still had no door. She slid the eggs onto the plate, then noticed a thin layer of sawdust now mixed with the butter and eggs.

"Damn," Anna said again, staring at the mess. "Gordon's got to get this done next week. This is ridiculous."

She took down another plate, rinsed it off and dried it with a paper towel. Then she lifted each egg with the spatula onto the clean plate, added buttered toast, and sat down to eat her slightly gritty breakfast, grumbling all the time about the state of the kitchen.

Emily came into the kitchen in her usual morning fog and put a cup of water into the microwave, then found the jar of instant coffee. Without thinking, Emily blew sawdust off the top of the jar before she opened it.

"He's got to finish up in here next week," Anna started. "We'll both be poisoned by ingesting wood chips if he doesn't."

Emily yawned. "I told Tammy I'd help her get the programs ready to go to the printer today. I probably won't be here when Gordon comes. If he comes today."

"Well, I'm leaving too, as soon as I finish my sawdust omelette," Anna said. "I'll leave him a note. I'll tell him you're going to hire someone else if he can't get this done next week."

"I would hire someone else, but Gordon's got all the cupboard doors at his house," Emily said. "Threaten him anyway, not that I think it'll speed him up. And tell him to pick up his tools too. I found a pair of pliers in my bathroom yesterday. I don't know what he was doing in there."

"We've been too easy with Gordon," Anna said. She rinsed off her plate and put it into the dishwasher. "You should never get friendly with the help."

"Not unless you can beat them at pinochle, right?" Emily asked.

Anna ignored her remark. "Marty called. You're supposed to call him back at the theater when you get up."

Emily nodded and sipped at her coffee. She hadn't heard from Marty for the past two days. Now she wondered what he wanted. Things were still a madhouse at the theater. The TNN crew was to arrive on Monday to get all their equipment in place for the live broadcast.

"I'm going to take my shower," Anna announced.

"Make it short because I need to shower as soon as you're finished," Emily said. Gordon also had not yet replaced the inadequate old water heater. "Mention the water heater in your note," Emily called after her mother.

Early in the afternoon, with both women still out, Gordon unlocked the back door of Emily's house and strolled into the kitchen. Rocko came up to rub his legs, and Gordon bent down and scratched the big cat behind the ears.

"Everyone gone?" Gordon asked the cat. He saw a note propped up on the counter and read it. "They won't hire anyone else." Rocko meowed in agreement. Gordon went back out and crossed the patio to the detached two-car garage. He switched on the ceiling light, and rummaged through an assortment of tools and paint cans on the workbench in the back of the garage. He went back in the house carrying a grooved wood chisel and several sheets of fine sandpaper.

For the next twenty minutes, Gordon sanded the edges of one of the lower cabinets. No remnants of the old white paint remained, and Gordon was pleased by the look of the wood's grain through the pecan stain and satin varnish he had applied last week. He sanded, then rubbed his fingers over the wood, sanded some more. He whistled softly, tunelessly. Rocko lay on the kitchen table, watching every move, then finally fell into a catnap.

In Emily's backyard, forty feet from the open back door, a figure with a baseball cap pulled low over his face squatted between two overgrown lilac bushes. He could hear Gordon whistling.

When Gordon had wiped the sawdust remnants from the rim of the cupboard, he straightened and stretched his back. Rocko watched him through slitted eyes. From a crumpled paper bag, Gordon took out two hinges and counted out screws. Using the chisel, Gordon removed a thin sheath of wood from the inner edge of the cupboard. He held up the hinge, then chiseled a bit more until the hinge fit flush with the wood's edge.

"The girls will be tickled when they get home," he told the cat.

Gordon stepped onto the sunny patio and shook out the dusting rag, whapping it against the leg of his overalls. The person in the bushes was motionless, invisible within the foliage. Gordon put the rag in his pocket and ambled across the patio and headed through the neighbor's backyard toward his own house, barely visible through the trees and bushes.

As soon as Gordon was out of sight, the man hiding in the lilacs moved quickly across the yard and through the open back door into Emily's kitchen. He looked at the cat on the table, but Rocko didn't move. He merely flattened his ears, and watched the intruder. The man pushed the ball cap back a bit on his forehead and took a quick look at the kitchen.

Moving into the hallway, he glanced into the living room, then quietly opened the door to Anna's downstairs bedroom. He scanned the room. Quickly rifled through the closet. Listened. There was no sound inside the house. He took the stairs three at a time. In Emily's bedroom, he looked at the bookshelves, pushed aside the clothes in her closet, unzipped the empty suitcase that still sat on the floor. Dropping to his knees, he looked under her bed. Nothing. In her office, he opened her desk drawers and filing cabinets. Listened again.

In the open door of the office, Rocko sat watching the man. The cat growled, startling the intruder. He turned and stared directly into the cat's eyes without a blink. Rocko retreated to a window-seat nook at the end of the hall, his tail twitching. He watched the man go downstairs and followed, but would go no further than the landing.

In the backyard, Gordon approached the patio carrying three cupboard doors. The warm pecan finish glistened in the sun. Gordon leaned the cupboard doors against the cabinet, picked up the chisel, and began whistling. Rocko knew the sound and came down the stairs. He stood outside the living room in the hallway and gave a loud, long caterwaul. The sound echoed off the high ceiling.

From the kitchen, Gordon called the cat's name. "Rocko? Where are you, boy?" In the living room, the intruder scanned the room for something heavy, blunt. But what he fixed on instead was the faded scrapbook laying on the coffee table. Again, the cat wailed as only a Siamese can.

Gordon came into the hallway, the chisel in one hand, a hinge in the other.

"What's the matter with you?" he asked the cat who continued to stare at the living room door. "There a mouse in there?"

Gordon walked past the cat into the living room. Out of the corner of his eye, Gordon saw a shadowy figure lunge toward him. But he saw the motion too late, and the attacker was on him from behind, his right arm around Gordon's throat, his left hand over Gordon's shoulder, pulling the arm tight. Gordon made a gurgling sound and stabbed at his assailant's arms with the chisel. The man cursed and knocked the chisel out of Gordon's hand, pulling tighter on his wrinkled throat. Now he had Gordon's feet off the floor, bouncing him as though he were shaking a pillow into a pillowcase. In the doorway, Rocko howled in one continuous plaintive cry. Gordon kicked and flailed, tearing at the man's arm around his throat. But the old man's strength was gone. A thin line of blood trickled down the attacker's left wrist where the chisel had gouged out a layer of flesh, then dripped onto

Gordon's chest. His face turned purple, his eyes bulged, and in a minute, he was dead.

The killer continued to hold the limp body for a few moments. Finally, he shifted his arm so he was holding Gordon around the chest. Gordon's head hung forward, his chin pressing against the killer's blood on his chest. Dragging Gordon with him to the coffee table, the killer reached down, and flipped open the scrapbook. A little smile curled his lips. Rocko crept under a chair in the hallway and crouched there silently.

The man picked up the scrapbook and hauled Gordon through the kitchen to the back door. At the door, he stopped and listened, stuck his head out, and surveyed the backyard. No one was in sight. Gordon's blank eyes were turned toward the pecan cupboards. The good ol' boy from Missouri, who had never left his home state, was nothing more than a burden to his assailant. Moments later, his crumpled body lay under the workbench where he had spent so many hours tinkering and fixing and whistling, undetectable beneath a paint-splattered drop cloth. The man in the ball cap was tying a rag around his bleeding wrist when a car pulled into the driveway.

The garage door opener came on, grinding as the door slowly rose. Crouched behind unpacked boxes, the wounded man clutched a pair of garden shears in his good hand. As the door rose, he could see a pair of high heels, then shapely legs draped in a loose summer dress. Emily walked in, so close that he could smell the perfume she had put on that morning. A ray of light fell across her face, and he could see the texture of her skin. He held his breath.

Emily surveyed the pile of boxes, then looked up at the shelves above. At the very top, she saw a box labeled REFERENCE. BRANSON MISC. She let out a groan and turned to get Gordon's stepladder, carrying it back to the pile of boxes. When she climbed the ladder, the killer could see right up her dress. As the muscles of her inner thighs tightened with each step, sweat poured down his face, burning his eyes. He thought of taking her, but he closed his eyes and bit down on the tip of his tongue. He had gotten what he came for.

With the box under her arm, Emily crossed the garage to the patio, looking at her keys, picking out the one for the back door. When she saw the open door, she stopped and called to Gordon. There was no answer. Emily walked into the kitchen cautiously. "Gordon?" she called again. "Rocko?" Emily saw the cupboard doors leaned against the counter. Maybe the note did the trick, she thought. She looked back out the kitchen door in the direction of Gordon's house. "He shouldn't just go off and leave the door open," she said with annoyance.

Emily carried the box upstairs to her office and sat it on the floor. She opened her filing cabinet and riffled through the labels until she found what she wanted. She closed the cabinet, took a quick glimpse at her answering machine and saw no messages, and went back down the stairs. In the hallway, she saw Rocko still crouched under the chair.

"What's the matter with you, Rocko?" Emily said. When the cat didn't move, Emily went out through the kitchen. From the patio she again called to Gordon, and watched in the direction of his house for a moment. She went to the back door, turned the lock, and pulled the door closed. "Hope he's got his keys," she muttered and went back through the garage and got in her car. She backed out of the driveway, and drove quickly down the street, not thinking to close the garage door.

The killer remained crouched behind the boxes for another three minutes. Slowly he stood up. He unwrapped the blood-stained rag from his hand and cursed quietly at the ugly gash. He walked to the front of the garage and looked down the street in both directions. Putting his injured hand in the pocket of his jeans, the man walked out of the garage and down the block to a faded black, slightly rusted pickup that was parked just around the corner. He got in and drove at a leisurely pace back to Emily's driveway. He backed in until the bed of the pickup was inside her garage. His movements would have aroused suspicion if anyone had been watching. But no one saw.

Quickly, listening for the sound of any approaching cars, he lifted Gordon's body into the pickup bed, pulling it forward behind the cab. He wrapped the drop cloth tightly around and under the dead man's body. He picked up the scrapbook from behind the boxes and tossed it on the bench seat, then pulled the truck out of the garage into the driveway. With the engine idling, he went back into the garage, pushed a button on the automatic door opener, and ducked out under it as it slowly closed. He didn't glance back at the house as he drove away. Somewhere nearby, someone started a lawn mower.

Inside, Rocko crept out from under the chair. He walked slowly into the living room, his toenails clicking on the hardwood floor. He went directly to the coffee table and pawed at something just under the edge. The wood chisel rolled out from under the table. Rocko sniffed delicately at the damp, bloody piece of flesh stuck in the chisel's groove.

☆ CHAPTER 14 ☆

"**H**ere's the file on sponsors of the benefit show," Emily said when she got back to Marty's office.

"Great," Tammy said. "I'll add these people to the invitation list. Free tickets for the first ten rows should make for an enthusiastic crowd when the camera pans."

"Everyone will be enthusiastic anyway," Emily said. "It's going to be a great show. Fourth of July's my favorite holiday. You don't have to buy presents for anyone, no sending out cards, and you get to see fireworks."

Tammy had a glum expression on her face. "What's the matter? You don't like fireworks?" Emily asked her.

"I was hoping for some fireworks last night with Stoney, but can you believe it? He wouldn't invite me back to his room. He said he was afraid he wouldn't be able to behave like the gentleman he is, and that I'd lose respect for him. How's that for a switch?"

"You should be grateful," Emily said. She was stuffing invitations into red, white, and blue envelopes. "How many other gentlemen have you dated lately?"

"I know," Tammy said, scratching her shoulder. "I'm not used to someone treating me with respect and consideration. That's a sad commentary, isn't it?"

Emily thought of Marty tucking her in and leaving her

to sleep on the lounger after his birthday party. She was even more certain now that it was best they hadn't made love. Things hadn't been right between them since that night, and making love would have made Emily feel even more confused. Right now, she felt more like a volunteer campaign worker than his girlfriend.

Her quick trip home crossed her mind, and she wondered out loud if she had closed the garage door. She couldn't remember doing it. She dialed the number of her house, but no one answered. She didn't think Gordon would answer the phone anyway, but with the liberties he seemed to be taking, she wasn't so sure. Apparently Anna wasn't home yet. She dialed Gordon's number, but he didn't answer there, either. Oh, well, she thought. Maybe I didn't leave it open. No great loss if someone steals some of Gordon's old tools anyway.

"So you had a good time with Stoney anyway?" Emily asked.

"Great," Tammy said, the dreamy quality returning to her eyes. "I can't believe how cool he is. He's got perfect manners, and he dresses great, and when he kissed me last night, I thought I was going to die."

"So he kissed you, but he wouldn't make love to you?" Emily said. "Did you ever hear the word *patience*?"

"I know, I know," Tammy said. "I'll be patient, or whatever else he wants me to be." She stuck her hand up under her sleeve and scratched. "He's supposed to call me this afternoon. I sure hope he wants to do something tonight. It'll be the first Saturday-night date I've had in about six months. Maybe some night the four of us could do something together."

Emily stopped stuffing envelopes and looked at Tammy. "You never suggested a double date before," she said. "That would be fun."

"I never had anybody good enough before," Tammy

said. "Besides, he and Marty are old friends."

"Have they gotten together yet?"

"No," Tammy said. "Stoney said he's not going to bother Marty until after the show Friday. That's the way he is."

"Tammy, what's the matter with you?" Emily asked. "Have you got chigger bites? You've been scratching all day."

Tammy's cheeks got pink, and she giggled. "You're going to think I'm a fool," she told Emily.

"Why? Have you been out dancing naked in the woods or something?"

"Promise you won't tell Marty? He'd think I was dumb," Tammy asked.

Now Emily was intrigued. "Tell me, or I'll tell Marty you've got a secret."

With a grin, Tammy rolled up her sleeve and loosened a small piece of gauze. "Look," she said.

Emily went over to her desk. There on Tammy's right shoulder was a small tattoo of a dagger. The skin around the tattoo was red where Tammy had been scratching.

"You got a tattoo?" Emily said. "I can't believe you'd do that. Why did you do that? And a dagger? Why not a rose?"

Tammy replaced the gauze and pulled down her sleeve, looking a little hurt. "I knew you'd think it was weird," she said.

"You're a big girl," Emily said, sorry she'd hurt Tammy's feelings. "You can get a tattoo if you want. At least it's a small one. But why a dagger?"

"Because Stoney's got one," Tammy said, pouting.

"Stoney's got a tattoo of a dagger?"

"Yeah. On his left hand," Tammy said. "Really, it's on his wrist. I saw it when his shirt cuff slid up while he was pouring my wine the other night."

"So because this new love of yours has a tattoo, you

run right out and get yourself marked for life? You've only been out with him three times. I can't believe you, Tammy."

Tammy scratched her shoulder. "I just thought it would be real neat the first time we make love if he discovers we have matching tattoos," Tammy said. "Don't you think he'll be impressed?"

"What if he thinks women shouldn't have tattoos? Maybe he'll think you look like some kind of mean biker chick."

Tammy looked very unhappy over this prospect. "You think so?" she lamented. "I never thought of that. Maybe I better not let him see it."

"Make love with the lights off for the rest of your life?"

"Shit," Tammy said. "It seemed like a good idea at the time."

"How much did it cost?"

"Forty-two dollars. Promise you won't tell Marty," Tammy implored.

"What's it worth to you?" Emily teased.

Tammy was lost in thought for a moment. Then she heard Emily's soft giggle. "You're just mean, Emily," Tammy said.

A voluptuous blond poked her head into the office. "Is Marty up here?" she asked.

"He's backstage," Tammy said. Emily recognized her as the woman at Marty's party who had wanted to sing with him.

"What's she doing here?" she asked Tammy when the woman was gone.

"Marty hired her yesterday," Tammy said.

"For what?"

"His fourth backup singer," Tammy said.

"He needs another backup singer?" Emily asked, feeling annoyed.

"I don't ask," Tammy said. "I just gave her an employment form to fill out."

"Did you hear her sing?"

"No," Tammy said. "You think Marty asks my opinion on everything?"

"What's her name?"

Tammy ruffled through a pile of papers in her inbasket and pulled one out. "Sherri Starr, with two *r*s," she said.

Emily snorted.

"She's twenty-three, from Lubbock, Texas, and she included her measurements in the margin of the form." Tammy slapped it back in the pile.

"I'm sure that's not why Marty hired her," Emily said sarcastically.

"I'm sure," Tammy agreed.

Over the next three hours, Emily and Tammy finished the invitations, got the press passes ready for the list of journalists who had applied to cover the event, and readied the program for the printer. They had constant interruptions. Several people came in asking where Marty was. The sound man came up with a list of equipment Tammy would have to rush order from Joplin. And the head costumer came in to pick up Sherri Starr's employment form.

"I hope her measurements are on here," the woman said, grabbing the form and bustling out.

"See?" Tammy said. "What do we know?"

By seven, the day's work was caught up, and Tammy announced she was going home. She'd grown increasingly glum as the hours passed without a call from Stoney. "Maybe he left me a message. I've been on the phone half the day, so he probably just called me at home," she said.

"Let's hope," Emily said to herself. Stoney still sounded too good to be true, but Emily hoped Tammy wouldn't be hurt by this guy. Especially after getting the tattoo.

After Tammy left, Emily stacked up the invitations she would take to the post office Monday and put them in her briefcase. She called the house to see if Anna wanted her to bring anything home from the grocery store, but there was no answer. Then she remember Anna's date with Tommy. She wondered if she should have told Marty, but that would have been too petty, like a kid telling tales to get someone else in trouble. Still, it made her a little nervous to think of Anna out with that man. But, after all, she did have her can of pepper spray.

Emily locked the office door and walked down the stairs. The cacophony of sounds that had drifted up all day from backstairs had ceased, and it was quiet backstage. Emily figured Marty was still there since he hadn't come up to tell them he was leaving, but she wasn't sure. She saw the costumer still bent over her desk in the wardrobe room. A stagehand passed, headed out the back door. Emily walked out to the rear of the stage. It always gave her an eerie feeling when the auditorium was empty and only a few backstage lights were on. Her footsteps echoed. She was still behind one of the wing curtains when she heard Marty laugh softly. Then a woman's giggle. Emily stopped, a feeling of foreboding seizing her chest like a meat hook. She could have called to him, but she didn't. Quietly, she walked forward until she rounded the edge of the curtain and could see out onto the stage. There was Marty, sitting on a stool, his guitar leaned against his leg. Also leaning against his leg was the new backup singer. Marty was kissing her. Emily's heart stopped. Marty had one arm slung around the woman's waist. Sherri Starr had her arms around Marty's neck. They stopped kissing, and Marty reached for his guitar. Emily couldn't hear what he said, but she could see his wide smile. Blood rushed to Emily's face, and she felt dizzy. Whatever feelings of sympathy she'd had for the man were gone. Whatever ideas of love and long relationships she'd had faded instantly, replaced by the blackness of betrayal and rejection. Emily slowly walked out of the wings onto the edge of the stage. The two turned to look at her. Marty stood up from the stool, brushing by the woman, and came toward her.

"Hi, honey," he said. "You and Tammy through upstairs?"

"You and I are through," she said, through clenched teeth.

Marty stopped in front of her. "What do you mean?" he said, sounding confused.

"You know what I mean," she said. With that, she turned and walked toward the backstage door.

"Wait a minute," he called after her, but she shoved open the door and slammed it behind her as hard as she could. She walked quickly toward her car, not stopping when she heard the door open. She didn't look back as she drove off.

The tears came when she was halfway home. She pounded on the steering wheel, cursing Marty through her sobs, cursing herself for being a fool, for believing he would be true to her, for fondly thinking they might be married someday. She had even fantasized about a wedding ceremony on the very stage where he had just kissed Sherri Starr.

"He's not for you," she told herself. "You should have known better. Everything's just for show."

By the time she pulled up to her garage, Emily had calmed herself down, determined that she was not going to let herself be hurt by this. After all, she'd done her best for Marty. His sleazy behavior was no reflection on her. It's just the way he was, and she would never believe now that he could change. She'd stood right there in the wings and seen him carrying on with some twenty-three-year-old bimbo. He knew she was still in the theater, upstairs working for him sans pay, stuffing his damn envelopes. Anger was replacing pain. She slammed the car door and slapped at the garage door closer.

In the house, Emily stomped through the rooms. She should have seen this coming the first night he stood her up for a date. She had let herself care, and this was the thanks she got. Marty didn't know how to deal with someone who cared. All he knew were users, and he'd just used Emily, too. She wanted to throw something. She wanted to scream. She stomped to the kitchen and nearly tripped over a cupboard door propped against the counter. She kicked the door, sending it skittering across the kitchen floor.

"Rocko," she yelled, the tears starting again. She sat at the kitchen table and sobbed for a minute, then with a force of will, she calmed herself and leaned back. Sadness at the lost possibilities for she and Marty crept in with her anger. She felt an ache deep inside. She knew it would be weeks, maybe months, before that ache went away.

She went to the refrigerator and opened a can of beer.

"Rocko?" she called again. She walked into the hallway, to call him again, thinking the cat was probably asleep on her bed. She heard the telephone ring and went into the living room. She caught herself before she answered the phone. Instead, she turned up the volume on her answering machine. "I can't come to the phone right now. Please leave me a message," Emily's recording said. Then there was the beep, then Marty's voice. "Call me. Please. I'll be at the house tonight." He hung up.

"Not a chance," she said quietly. She saw Rocko curled up near the coffee table, and went over to scratch his head.

"Why didn't you come to greet me tonight?" she asked the cat. "You deserting me too?" Then she saw the chisel resting beside the cat's paw. She picked it up and stood up. "That's it for Gordon," she said angrily, carrying the chisel to the kitchen and laying it on the counter. "He goes off and leaves my door open. He leaves his tools all over the house and nothing gets fixed." Tears welled in her eyes again as she leaned against the counter. Her eyes rested on the chisel and she noticed a red stain on the blade.

"Probably gouged himself and decided to take the rest of the day off. Probably wants workman's compensation."

Emily stomped upstairs and took a shower. That made her feel a little better, so she fixed herself an avocado sandwich and curled up on the couch with a new copy of *Traveler* magazine. Rocko snuggled beside her.

Emily jolted awake to the sound of the front door slamming. "Mom?" she called.

"Yes," Anna said. She walked into the living room. "I broke up with Tommy," she said. Her eyes were blazing, and she slammed her purse down on the bar. "He's a jerk." Anna plopped into a chair.

"What'd he do?" Emily asked, pushing Rocko onto the floor. "Are you all right?"

"I'm fine," Anna said, her mouth set in a thin line. "He admitted he'd tried to botch things for Marty at TNN," she said. "Can you believe it? And then he had the nerve to try to get me to talk to Marty and fix things up between them! He's a conniving old fool, and I'm not having another thing to do with him."

Anna looked closer at Emily. "What's the matter with you?"

"Caught Marty kissing his new backup singer," Emily said.

"No!" Anna said.

"Told him we were through," Emily added.

The two women looked at each other. A smile crept

across Anna's face, then Emily's.

"We're a couple of fools, you know it?" Anna said. "Let's make an oath. No more men."

"Sounds good to me," Emily said. "Want to drive down to Blue Eye tomorrow and go to the flea markets?"

"Absolutely. Let's see if Tammy wants to go," Anna said, reaching for the phone. "It's only ten thirty. She'll still be up."

"She was supposed to have a date with Stoney tonight," Emily said. "She's probably still out."

Anna listened while the phone rang at Tammy's.

"I thought you'd be out tonight," Anna said when Tammy answered. "Well, don't worry about it. You're better off that he didn't call. Emily and I have agreed we're through with men. We're going junking in Blue Eye tomorrow, and we're going to spend the day talking about what rats men are. Want to come with? Great. We'll pick you up at noon."

"Stoney didn't call her," Anna said when she'd hung up. "Tammy said now she was stuck with a stupid dagger. What did she mean by that?"

Daggers, Emily thought. Tammy has one on her arm, I've got one in my heart, and Mother . . .

Seeming detached, with wide eyes, Anna chirped, "Cheesecake?"

Emily looked up at her with a little smile and nodded. And Mother, she thought. How good to have this special, eccentric woman back in my life.

⋆ CHAPTER 15 ⋆

By noon on Monday, there was still no sign of Gordon. They hadn't seen him Sunday either, although his truck had been parked in his driveway all weekend.

"Now I'm starting to worry," Anna said.

"I'm sure he went off on a fishing trip with some crony, or maybe he's on a weekend binge," Emily said. She had just returned from the post office where she had mailed the invitations to Marty's show. She had debated whether or not to chuck them in the trash can, but had decided that just because he was a rat, it was no reason for her to stoop to his level. He'd called twice on Sunday asking her to call him, but Emily had screened her calls. A clean break was the best way. During the shopping jaunt the day before with Anna and Tammy, Emily had some melancholy thoughts about the good times she and Marty had had. But the women had managed to comfort each other. Emily decided she was suffering more from disillusion than true heartbreak.

"I'm going down to his house," Anna said.

Fifteen minutes later, she was back. "I think something's wrong," she said. "His door's not locked."

"That's probably not unusual," Emily said. "He went off on Saturday and left our back door open. I came home to get a file, and there it was, gaping wide open and no sign of Gordon. I shouted for him. Then I locked it when I left. I don't think he ever came back inside because these cabinet doors were laying here when I left and were in the same spot when I came home. What time did you get home Saturday?"

"I came back about three, but Gordon wasn't here then, and the back door was locked."

"Was the garage door down?" Emily asked. "I thought I had forgotten to close it when I went back to the office."

Anna thought about it. "It was down when I got home because I had to look for the opener. It had slid back under my seat. Maybe Gordon closed it."

"I bet his keys are somewhere in the house here, and he couldn't get back in on Saturday, so he went off with someone else."

"No," Anna said. "His keys are on his kitchen table."

"You went in?"

"Well, he's in our house all the time," Anna said. "It's not like I was over there snooping."

"So what's it like?"

"Like a sixty-five-year-old's bachelor pad," Anna said. "Dishes in the sink, clothes on the floor, a trash can full of empty beer cans. His wallet was on the table, too. Why would he go somewhere without his wallet? Maybe we should call the police."

"And tell them what?" Emily asked. "I'm sure they're not going to issue a missing person's report on Gordon."

"Well, he's missing, isn't he?" Anna said. "And what's the matter with Rocko? He won't come out of the living room. I don't think he's even eaten. Maybe we should take him to the vet."

"He *has* been acting weird," Emily said. Then she thought of the chisel she had found beside Rocko. It still lay where she had put it on the counter with some of Gordon's other tools. Emily picked it up and looked at it more closely. "Does this look like blood to you?" she asked Anna.

Anna came over and looked at it, too. "I think it's blood," she said. "That could even be a little skin on it. Maybe he hurt himself. I should call the hospital."

Emily went in the living room and picked up the cat. She examined him, but found no hint of a wound. When she put him down, he curled up again near the coffee table. "Talk to me, Rocko." But the cat said nothing.

"Well, he's not in the hospital," Anna said. "I'm calling the police."

"Go ahead," Emily said, "but they're not going to pay any attention to you."

A few minutes later, Anna came back in. "They're coming over. I told them about the chisel."

The two Branson patrolmen listened to the women patiently, but as Emily had predicted, they reassured her that Gordon had probably left with someone and would be back soon. They did take the chisel with them, without any show of alarm. One officer dropped it into a plastic bag. They asked Emily if anything was missing in the house. She had noticed nothing amiss, she told them. Anna was annoyed that they didn't offer to search for Gordon. But by late afternoon, neither the women nor the police were giving the matter much thought. Emily had been working on her magazine article, and Anna had gone to the grocery store.

At four o'clock, Emily's telephone rang, and she listened to the incoming message, hoping it wouldn't be Marty. But the caller identified himself as Sheriff Crockett from Wimberley. Emily picked up the phone.

"I called Marty's office," the sheriff said. "But he wasn't available. His secretary told me you were his girlfriend. I guess you weren't putting me on."

Emily wasn't sure how to answer, but she wanted to know why the sheriff was calling so she didn't mention the recent trouble with Marty.

"We've had some breaking developments," the sheriff said, "and I think Marty needs to know. We're keeping it quiet here as long as we can, but I don't know how long it'll be until the press picks up on this. We got back the lab results from Austin. Forensics says that Chick died as a result of a stab wound to the back of his neck. Penetrated his brain stem. It was something small, maybe an ice pick. And it looks like he was killed on the ground, not on his roof. Evidence shows there were bruises to the roots of his hair in the front of his head. Someone held him by the hair and pounded his head against those bricks in the rose bed. Probably after he was dead."

Emily sat down, stunned. The brutality of it shocked her.

"Who did it?" she asked.

"We've got no clues," he said. "We've searched the property, but there's no weapon, no footprints, nothing. None of the neighbors saw anything unusual. And no one's come up with any motive for why someone would want him dead. Except me." The sheriff's voice sounded strained, as though he were in pain.

"What do you mean?"

There was a pause. "I'm not sure I have any business telling you this.

"If there's any way Marty could be in danger, you have to tell me."

"I do have some concerns," the sheriff said. "Not that I think he is in danger, but he needs to know."

"What?" Emily asked.

"We do have a suspect. After the day I met you, I got to thinking. I called the warden at Huntsville. Cole McCay was released from prison three days before Chick was killed."

"As I asked you in Wimberley, Sheriff, what has this got to do with Marty? I think you'd better fill me in. Why would Cole want to hurt Chick or Marty?"

"Because they sent him to prison," the sheriff said. "They turned him in, and they testified against him. When the verdict was read, McCay stood up in the courtroom and cursed them and swore he'd get revenge."

"How could they have released him?" Emily asked.

"His sentence was thirty years to life. It's been thirty years. Texas prison are overcrowded, and he's been a model inmate, the warden said. He was only nineteen at the time of the murder. The warden said three psychologists testified to the parole board that he's been completely rehabilitated."

"Then why do you suspect he's the one that killed Chick?" Emily asked.

The sheriff paused. It was hot in his office, and he rubbed his hand over his sweaty face. "Because I was in the courtroom that day. I was looking right into his eyes when he swore revenge. And I never saw anyone look more evil."

Outside Emily's window, the sun went behind a cloud.

"And there's one more thing," Crockett said. "McCay's skipped probation. No one knows where he is."

Without thinking, Emily scanned the wooded backyard visible from the window of her office.

"Isn't anyone looking for him?" she asked.

"There's a A.P.B. filed on him for breaking parole, but like I said, there's no evidence to connect him to Chick's death. But we will bring him in for questioning if we can find him."

Emily's head was spinning. She didn't know if she should be afraid or not. She did know she would have to see Marty now. He had to hear this.

"What should we do, Sheriff?" Emily asked.

The sheriff pulled on his thick eyebrow. "If I had Marty's money, I'd hire the biggest bodyguards I could find," the sheriff said. "The only trouble is, they wouldn't know who to look for."

"What do you mean?"

"Well, it seems that the prison hasn't been so consistent in updating mug shots," the sheriff said. "The last photo we've got of McCay is from thirty years ago. We don't know what he looks like now."

Emily thanked the sheriff for the call. She dialed Tammy's number right away, before she lost her nerve. She told Tammy that it was an emergency, that she had to talk to Marty immediately.

Tammy started to needle her about losing her resolve to break up with him, but something in Emily's voice told Tammy this was indeed serious.

Fifteen minutes later, Emily answered the phone on the first ring. It was Marty.

"Hi, baby," he said. "I'm so glad you called. We've got to talk about this whole thing. It's not what it looked like, and I'm going crazy without you."

Emily kept her voice as cold as she could even though part of her longed to forget the scene she'd seen onstage.

"I have to see you right away," she said. "It's about Chick and Cole McCay, and you have to listen to me this time. Chick was stabbed with an ice pick, and Cole's out of prison."

There was a long silence on the phone. "I'll come right over," Marty said finally.

When Marty walked through Emily's door, his face was pale. He came toward her with his arms out, but Emily put her hand forward.

"No, Marty," Emily said. "Just listen to me."

Emily told him everything about going to the Wimberley newspaper, meeting the sheriff, and this afternoon's phone call. As she talked, she saw a light veil of perspiration form on Marty's face. When she had finished, Marty asked if she had any whiskey in the house.

Emily brought him a double shot of bourbon in a small tumbler, and Marty took a big swallow. The liquor seemed to bring a little color back to his face.

"Why are you so afraid of this guy?" Emily finally asked. "Look at you."

Marty took another sip, and slicked back his hair. He cleared his throat.

"Because I saw what he did that night," he said.

"You saw him kill the girl?" Emily asked.

Marty looked at her through narrowed eyes. "You're just dying to hear about it, aren't you?" There was anger in his voice. "All right. I'll tell you what you've been wanting to know. Maybe then you'll understand why I've been trying to protect you. You don't think I care about you because you saw me kissing that girl. That didn't mean a damn thing to me, and it didn't go any further than that. But you think it was some big deal. You think everything should be black and white, plain and simple. Well, life ain't that way, Emily. You're a dreamer. Sometimes things go haywire, and you make a mistake you regret for the rest of your life. That's what happened on Devil's Ridge."

Marty got up and paced out into the hallway, then came back and sat down on the couch across from Emily.

"We'd just finished a gig in Comal County. The Cadillac Cowboys. Me, Chick, and Cole. Cole was two years older than us. He'd come from Georgia and was new in town. He heard us play one night and said he'd like to play with us. Our other guitar player had just been drafted. We listened to him, and he was so good it made your hair tingle. And God Almighty, what a voice. He'd been with us three months. He was pretty much a loner, and he'd been around a lot more than us. But he showed up on time and the Cowboys had never sounded so good.

That night, we got a case of beer after the gig. At the liquor store, we ran into Shirley Mullen. She'd been a couple years ahead of us in high school, but we knew her. She was a real friendly girl. Some people in town thought she was loose. A lot of people shunned her for how she dressed and acted, but Chick and I had always liked her. I don't know what she did on the side, and I never cared. We asked her if she wanted to go party with us up at the swimming hole, and she said she would. She and Cole hit it off right away. He had a way of attracting the women. We didn't understand what it was about him, but we thought it was kind of cool."

Marty stopped and looked at Emily, whose face showed no emotion.

"So by the time the case was about gone, Cole and Shirley take off up the trail for a walk. Chick and I sat there giggling like a couple of twelve-year-olds talking about wet dreams."

Marty finished the whiskey in his glass. "We heard her scream. The first scream, we just went into fits of laughter, picturing some kind of spectacular sex. But she kept screaming, and we knew something horrible was happening. We ran down the trail, following the sound of her screams. We came up over a ridge, and we saw them off the trail about fifty feet under some trees. Cole was on top of her."

Marty was staring into space. "He was stabbing her, and she wasn't screaming anymore. He must have stabbed her half a dozen times while we stood there, just paralyzed. Then one of us must have made a noise because he turned around and looked at us over his shoulder. He waved at us with his hunting knife."

Marty put his head in his hands and rubbed his forehead.

Emily sat motionless, watching him. When he looked

up at her, she could see the horror of the scene in his eyes.

"We ran," he said. "We turned tail and ran back to the truck and peeled out of there. It must have been a half hour before we could even talk about it. Halfway back to Wimberley, we turned around and went back. We snuck down that trail like theives. Cole was gone, of course. And so was Shirley. Some kids found her body a couple of days later. He'd stabbed her and then thrown her off a cliff right beside the trail. It took us a few more days to work up our courage to call the sheriff and tell him what we'd seen. Chick and I never talked about what happened that night. And we never sang together again. But I knew by looking in his eyes every time I saw him that we would always share that guilt. There were two of us, Emily. We might have been able to stop him. She might not have been dead yet. We might have been able to get her help."

Marty leaned back on the couch and looked at his hands. "We killed her as much as Cole did. We could have done something, but we ran. It was real hard to say that at the trial."

Emily went over and sat beside him. She put her hand on his knee. She didn't know what to say. There was no sympathy she could offer; no strength that could lift his burden.

"Now he's got Chick," Marty said quietly. "Maybe the best thing is to let him get me too."

Emily ignored the remark.

"Why do you think he did it?"

Marty shook his head. "I don't know. I've always thought he was raping her and she was resisting. Even then, I can't understand what kind of rage would make someone do something like that."

"You need to hire extra security right away," Emily said.

"If he was going to come after me, why wouldn't he have tried something already?" Marty said. "Maybe it wasn't Cole who killed Chick."

"Don't take any chances," Emily said. "Surely they'll pick him up for something and get him back behind bars where he should be. But you need to be careful until he's caught."

"I'll get some extra boys in there until Friday anyway," Marty said. "Nothing's interrupting the show."

Marty took her hand. "What about you and me?" he asked.

"What about you and Miss Starr?" Emily asked.

"Here's the way it was," Marty said. "She was so happy I'd hired her, and so excited about being in the show, she just got overcome, I guess. She just grabbed me and kissed me. And that's when you walked in. It just didn't mean anything. Are you going to forgive me?"

Despite everything that had happened, she still felt an attachment to Marty. He'd just sat there and told her about a horrible mistake he'd made thirty years ago. It made his mistake with Sherri Starr seem terribly insignificant. Emily felt confused.

"Look," she said. "I don't mean to complicate your life right now. I was hurt by what I saw, but let's put everything on hold for right now. Let's make sure you're safe, let's get the show over, and then we'll sit down and talk about where we stand. All I've ever wanted is for you to be honest with me."

He slid his arm around her shoulders and pulled her against his shoulder, resting his head against her hair. She allowed the embrace because it felt good. She wanted to believe everything would somehow work out. He was right. She was a dreamer.

☆ CHAPTER 16 ☆

The day felt like the first of July. Steam rose from the lakes as the sun came up to heat the muggy air. Early fishermen had to take it slow in the mist, their bass boats barely leaving a wake in the silver water. By noon, it was ninety-two degrees. Along the strip, kids screamed as they plummeted down water slides, and bungee jumpers sweated while they waited in line for the thrill of their lives.

Emily sat in Marty's office and listened to him lying to Jack Wells, the owner of Guardian Security. Marty told the small, wiry man with thinning hair that he thought a disgruntled former stagehand was behind the threatening calls he'd been getting for the past two weeks. Marty said he thought the guy might have followed him home the night before. That's why he had called the security company, he said. And he made sure that Wells understood the importance of the live Fourth of July show that would be broadcast on Friday night. Millions of viewers nationwide watching Marty Rose, he said. And millions of dollars rolling into town when all those viewers planned their next vacation. If the show were marred by some nutcase, Branson's image could be damaged.

"That could put us all out of business, you understand," Marty told him.

Wells seemed impressed by the seriousness of the predicament, undoubtedly thinking about his own business's future—just as Marty had intended.

"And you do understand that your men have to be low key?" Marty asked him. "This show is live from Branson where life is one big vacation, and there's no crime to worry about. That's exactly how it's got to look both to the audience in my theater and to everyone watching at home. No one in uniform, no guns showing, no hassling the customers, no disruptions of any sort. I'm not expecting any trouble, and I don't expect any from your team. Got it?"

"Prevention is the name of the game for us." Wells gave him a reassuring smile. "My men are bodyguards for half the stars in town, but you'd never know it. They're trained to be invisible and make sure troublemakers don't even get close to starting anything. We'll make sure the guy doesn't get anywhere near you."

Guardian would assign four men to the case, he told Marty. One would be posted at the theater's back entrance, checking to be certain everyone entering the theater was authorized. Two would work the lobby. One would guard the front gate of Marty's home and patrol the grounds.

Wells made notes on a legal pad. "I'll need you to show me the layout of the theater and get someone to show me around your home and the grounds," he said. "I'll get the guys out here as soon as we're finished and brief them on the situation. Everything will be in place by late this afternoon."

He asked Marty how long the suspect had worked backstage, why he'd been fired, and said he'd need to check his employment record for an address and other identification. Marty made up vague answers, admitting that the stagehand hadn't provided much information before they'd had to fire him for getting in a fight with another employee.

"He was just hired to move scenery," Marty said. "We didn't care about his life history."

"Well, he probably wouldn't have given you correct information anyhow. Sounds like the kind of drifter we're seeing a lot of these days," Wells said. "Give me a description of this guy."

Marty glanced at Emily who waited to see how he would handle this question. She knew Marty wasn't about to tell the security man the truth. He had talked to Tammy and Emily about it that morning and had made it clear to both of them that if word got out that a killer was stalking Marty Rose it could cause adverse publicity. If anyone tracked the story back to Chick's death, Marty's image as a good-time country singer could take a serious hit.

Marty hadn't gone into the full story in front of Tammy. He'd only said that a guy named Cole McCay had killed someone and that he and Chick had testified against him. He told Tammy that McCay might be implicated in Chick's death. So Marty was presenting a false scenario to the security firm. That could hinder their ability to protect him, but on this question of the man's description, Emily knew Marty couldn't give the security man any help. He hadn't seen Cole McCay for thirty years.

"He's about six feet tall. He's got kind of curly hair, dark brown. He's slim, but fairly muscular," Marty said. "I'd say he was in his midforties. His face was kind of pale."

Emily watched the skin around Marty's eyes tighten as he tried to picture an older Cole McCay. He must have been thinking of life in prison when he mentioned pale skin.

"Is there anything else you can tell us about the guy that could identify him?" Wells asked.

Marty thought for a minute. "He's got a deep voice and his accent doesn't sound like he's from around here," Marty said. "I think he said once that he'd come up from Georgia."

Tammy dropped her cup of coffee and it hit the table in front of the couch where she sat taking notes, sending a stream of coffee dripping onto the carpeting. The security man jumped at the sound.

"I'm sorry," Tammy apologized. "Clumsy of me."

Emily noticed that Tammy had a strange expression on her face as she mopped the spilled coffee with wads of tissue and dabbed at the puddle on the carpet. She was acting like she was frightened, but Emily didn't understand why. Maybe her overprotective feelings for Marty had made her nervous.

"All right," said Wells. "I'll need a list of everyone authorized to be backstage."

"Get that for us, Tammy," Marty said. "Leave the damn rug."

Tammy got the list from her desk and handed it to Wells. He ran his finger slowly down the list.

"There's no address listed for this Stoney Barnes," he said to Marty. "Who's he?"

"Stoney Barnes?" Marty said, frowning. "The name's not ringing a bell. Who is that, Tammy?"

Tammy was still daubing at liquid that had run into the groove in the coffee table. "He's that old friend of yours who stopped by last week," Tammy said, not looking up. "Remember I told you about him?"

"Stoney Barnes?" Marty said again. "I don't remember anyone by that name." He looked at Tammy and waited for an explanation.

"He's the guy that came by last Tuesday when you were in Nashville," Tammy said. "I told you about him.'' She was sounding more defensive with Marty than Emily had ever heard.

"Why's he on the backstage list?'' Marty asked.

"He's the guy I've been dating,'' Tammy said through clenched teeth. "Was dating,'' she corrected. "He was going to come to the show with me, and I thought it'd be easier for him if he had a backstage pass.'' She glared at Marty. "He's not the stagehand you fired,'' she said pointedly.

"Well, that's just great,'' Marty said, glaring back at Tammy. "Why don't you invite the whole damn town into my dressing room for a little party? Hey, anybody out there know Marty Rose? Come on in.'' Marty waved his arms.

Tammy sat silent, picking at the remnants of glue on one fingernail.

"Do you know where Mr. Barnes lives?'' Wells asked Tammy.

"No,'' she said, pouting like a scolded child.

"You give some guy a backstage pass, and you don't even know where he lives?'' Marty asked.

"He's a nice guy,'' Tammy said. Emily thought her voice quavered a little. "He was going to meet me here.''

Marty looked at Wells. "Tell your man to escort him to my office when he gets here,'' he said. "I'll be glad to see my *old friend*,'' Marty said, turning his gaze on Tammy, who had slumped lower into the couch cushions as though she wanted to disappear.

Suddenly, Emily remembered the scrapbook. She didn't know why she hadn't thought to mention it to Marty the night before. Even though she had seen no clues in those dry pages, Marty might have found something she had overlooked.

Wells went over a few more details with Marty, and Marty signed his contract. He called backstage and had one of the techs come upstairs to escort Wells on a tour of the theater. As soon as Wells left, Tammy headed out of the office too.

"I'm going to the ladies room," she announced before she slammed the office door.

Emily raised an eyebrow at Marty. "Why were you so tough on Tammy?" she asked. "She gave him that pass not knowing there was any security problem."

Marty rubbed his temples. "I know. I'm just a little edgy."

"We all need to stay calm," Emily said. "After the show, we can all relax."

"I can't relax until McCay's back behind bars," Marty snapped. "There have been too many people dying around me lately. I don't care how many guards I hire, I'm the only one who's going to recognize him. I'm going to have to be watching my back every second from now on."

Emily hesitated to tell Marty about the scrapbook. She didn't look forward to the same scolding attitude that he'd turned on Tammy. But he had to know.

"There's something I've been meaning to tell you about," she began. She explained that Nita had given her the scrapbook, and that she had intended to give it to Marty as soon as she got back.

"But when I was telling you about my trip to Texas, you said you didn't want to think about the past anymore," she said. "And you've been so distracted by the show that I decided I'd wait and give it to you next week. Last night there was so much going on, I never thought about it."

Tammy came back into Marty's office while Emily was talking. It must have been apparent to Tammy from Emily's tone that she was afraid of being called on the carpet too.

Tammy tried to lighten the situation, surprising Emily by coming to her defense.

"It's got some really cool pictures of you," Tammy said. "I love the 1960s sideburns. You ought to grow them back."

"You saw the scrapbook?" Marty asked.

"Yeah, over at Emily's," Tammy said, realizing that she shouldn't have opened her mouth.

"That's swell," Marty said sarcastically. "Maybe you girls would like to open the Marty Rose museum. Who else saw it?" he asked Emily.

She hadn't meant for anyone else to see it, and now she felt guilty, like she had invaded his privacy.

"Just Tammy and mom," Emily said. "There's nothing embarrassing to you in the scrapbook. I'm sure Chick meant it as a tribute to you."

"Would you mind going home and getting it?" he asked Emily coldly.

"Not at all," she said. She left the office without a word.

Driving back to her house, Emily fumed. Marty's mood was understandable, but that was no excuse for being rude and childish. She would hang in there for three more days. But once the show was over and the pressure was off Marty, she wasn't going to continue the relationship. She felt pretty certain of that.

Anna was in the living room watching a gardening show on PBS. The scrapbook was not on the coffee table.

"Where's Marty's scrapbook?" Emily asked.

"I don't know," Anna said. "I didn't take it."

Emily couldn't remember moving it, but she went upstairs and looked in her bedroom and her office. Back in the living room, she said, "I can't find it. Are you sure you didn't put it someplace?"

"I'm not going senile, Emily," Anna said. "The last time I saw it was right here when Tammy and I were looking through it before we went to the garage sales. What day was that?"

"I thought you weren't getting senile," Emily said. "It was Friday."

"That was the last day we saw Gordon," Anna said.

Emily rummaged through a pile of newspapers on the end table.

"You don't think Gordon took it, do you?" Anna asked.

"Why would Gordon take it? What value would that scrapbook possibly have to anyone but Marty?"

There was no answer to Emily's question. Anna got up and began to look around the house. Emily went back upstairs for a more intensive search. While she was in her office, she noticed the envelope that contained the rose from the scrapbook. She dumped it out. It had dried. The petals were crisp and the spot of mold just powder. An unpleasant odor still clung to the blossom.

After searching every possible place the scrapbook could have been, Emily took the envelope with the rose and went back to the theater.

"I can't find the scrapbook," she told Marty. "I can't understand what happened to it. This was tucked into the scrapbook." She handed Marty the envelope.

Marty looked inside. He frowned and wrinkled his nose and dumped the rose out onto his desk.

"When Nita gave me the scrapbook, the rose wasn't dried out. She must have picked it in Chick's rose garden for you," Emily said.

Marty picked up the dried bloom and stared at it. He looked at Emily.

"Were there pictures of Cole in the scrapbook?" he asked.

"No," Emily said. "I thought it was weird when I looked through it. He'd been cut out of all the pictures."

"It wouldn't help anyway," Marty said. "He had long sideburns back then too. He's probably gray or bald by now." He turned the rose over in his hand.

"This came from Chick's garden?" he asked Emily.

"I don't know," she said. "That's what I assumed."

"Didn't Nita say why she'd put it in there?" Marty asked.

"I didn't ask Nita about the rose," Emily said slowly and deliberately. "I didn't even notice it until I was back at my motel. I didn't think it mattered. It's just a rose. It could have come from the arrangement you had Tammy send. Why are you so concerned about it?"

Marty got up and went to a sideboard where an insulated pitcher of coffee sat. He lifted the pot, then sat it down too hard.

"Tammy, get the cafe to send up some fresh coffee."

Tammy went to her office without a word, and Emily heard her pick up the phone.

"When I was in Nashville," Marty said quietly to Emily, "the cops told me that there was a rose in Zach's pocket when they found him. I told you that, didn't I?"

"Yes," Emily said. "You thought Tommy was responsible for that, to implicate you. What's that got to do with this?"

Marty picked up his phone and dialed information. "I guess I'm going to have to find out," he said. "Wimberley. County clerk's office."

Emily listened as Marty talked to Nita, offering his condolences and talking about the horror of the coroner's findings. He didn't mention Cole McCay.

"Well, that must be nice to have your son home with you," Marty told Nita. "I wanted to thank you for the scrapbook. It brought back a lot of memories," he lied. "I was wondering about the rose in it."

After a few more minutes, Marty hung up. "The rose was in Chick's shirt pocket when Nita found him," he said.

Emily couldn't think how the two could be connected.

"Cole never even knew Zach, did he?"

Marty shut the office door, leaving Tammy scowling at the closed door. He came over and sat heavily on the couch beside Emily.

"When Cole was with the Cowboys, he wrote a song. It was a damn good one. The only problem was that, well, let's just say some of the lyrics couldn't be played in public. Chick and I tinkered with it, put in some new lyrics, and changed a few chords here and there. Hell, Cole didn't seem to mind. He just liked having 'his song' performed." A couple years later, he was in prison and I was in Nashville, trying to convince Zach to take me on as a client. I needed a heavy-hitter agent, and I needed a great song to get his attention. I took him a demo tape I had recorded of 'Two Hearts Tied'."

Emily waited for him to go on, but he just sat there twirling the dried rose between his fingers.

"So?" she asked. "What's that got to do with anything?"

"I told Zach everything; that Cole wrote it and that Chick and I changed things a little. He said the hell with Cole, the song belonged to me and Chick."

"You stole Cole's song? Is that what you're saying?" Emily asked.

"That's it," Marty said. He tossed the rose onto the coffee table. One petal broke off.

"I don't understand," Emily said. "Cole was in prison. How would he have known you took credit for some song you played for Zach?"

Marty got up and walked to the line of gold records hanging behind his desk. He pointed to one of them and looked at Emily.

"'Two Hearts Tied'," he said. "Zach wanted to publish it. I dragged my feet. I tried to talk him into letting me record other songs, but he was set on that one. I talked to Chick about it, and he said that it was as much our song as it was Cole's. And he was right because if we hadn't made the changes, that song never would have been put on paper. So I did it. Copyrighted it and recorded it. Chick was on the label as cowriter. I was just hoping it would get me a steady job at some club.''

Marty popped a knuckle on his right hand.

"Two weeks later, I heard it play on Nashville's biggest station. It hit the charts and climbed to number one in three weeks and stayed there for three months. Every station in the country was playing it a dozen times a day. And every time I heard that song on the radio, I thought about Cole.''

Emily was shocked. She could understand someone wanting revenge on the friends who sent him to prison for life. But now Emily could picture Cole lying on a dirty mattress in a hot Texas jail and hearing his song come on the radio. His song. Maybe writing that song was the only thing he'd ever been proud of doing. And Marty Rose was getting the credit, the money, and the fame.

"Did you ever hear from Cole after the song came out?" Emily asked.

Marty went and sat down behind his desk. "Zach got a letter from a lawyer one day. About six months after the song came out. The lawyer said 'Two Hearts Tied' was Cole's song and that he wanted fifty thousand dollars.''

"Did you pay him?''

"Hell, no," Marty said with a snort. "He was in prison for life. What was he going to do with fifty thousand dollars? And what was I supposed to do? Tell my fans that an old friend of mine, who, by the way, folks, is in prison because he's a vicious killer, actually wrote my biggest hit?''

Marty drummed on his desk with a pencil. "Besides, there wasn't any way he could prove he'd written it. You think anyone in Wimberley was going to testify for Cole?

Zach threw the letter in the trash, and that's the last we heard of it.''

"Until two weeks ago," Emily said quietly.

Marty threw the pencil across the room where it bounced soundlessly on the plush carpet. "And until the day Chick died," Marty said defensively, "I split every cent I ever made off that song with him. Chick had enough for a down payment on that house, he always managed to have a nice pickup truck, and that money's still sending his boys to college."

Emily could think of nothing to say. She wanted to get out of the theater and away from Marty. Luckily, Tammy picked that moment to buzz Marty's intercom.

"Mr. Wells is back to see you," she said. Her voice was flat and formal.

"I'll be out in a minute," Marty snapped.

"Look," Emily said, standing up and edging toward the door. "I'm going to go home. I'll look again for the album. I'm sure it was just put away somewhere. I'll call you when I find it."

She was almost through the door when Marty caught up with her and put his hand on her shoulder. She turned her head toward him and saw the sheepish look on his face, an apology and a plea for understanding on his lips, but she kept moving into the outer office where Mr. Wells stood paging through his legal pad. Emily kept walking and didn't even speak to Tammy.

When she opened the door to the parking lot, the thick, suffocating air hit her like a blast from a furnace. Hurrying to her car, she walked past an older couple standing near their car. They were looking at the tickets they apparently had just purchased.

"Seventh row!" the woman said. "Those will be great seats."

"Yeah," the man answered with a touch of sarcasm. "We'll be able to see Marty Rose sweat."

☆ CHAPTER 17 ☆

Emily didn't call Marty. By Wednesday morning, she still hadn't found the scrapbook even though she and Anna had both searched again Tuesday night. She wasn't convinced she would have called Marty even if she'd found it. His confession about the song had left a bad taste in her mouth. She understood that he'd been young and was pushing hard to be successful. But it left Emily wondering if Marty wasn't just an outright thief.

The only explanation for the missing album that either of the women could come up with was that Gordon must have taken it. Maybe he'd planned to go off with some pals and had thought he'd borrow the album to show it to them, Anna said. Emily thought that was unlikely, but she didn't argue. Anna was already upset, torn between worrying about the missing handyman and being angry he'd left without any word to them.

About noon, Tammy called. "I'm on my lunch hour, and I wondered if I could stop by and talk to you," she asked Emily.

"How are things at the theater?" Emily asked Tammy when she arrived.

"Horrible," Tammy said as she set down her purse

and gave Anna a hug. "Marty's on the warpath. I've never seen him so uptight."

"I heard he was kind of rough on you yesterday," Anna said.

"I'm not alone," Tammy said. "The people backstage are at the point of revolt." Her face grew serious. "Can I sit down? This is all making me so nervous. And can I get a glass of water?"

Anna herded Tammy into the kitchen and seated her at the table, then got her a glass of ice water.

"When Marty was describing the phoney stagehand to Mr. Wells yesterday, I assumed he was kind of describing what Cole McCay looks like, at least as he remembered him."

"So did I," Emily said. "But that was thirty years ago. A person could change a lot in thirty years."

"But he said the man talked with a Georgia accent," Tammy said. She wiped at the condensation forming on her glass of water with her finger.

"So?" Emily prodded. "What about it?"

"Stoney told me he was from Georgia," Tammy said.

"A lot of people are from Georgia," Anna said. "Why are you worrying about that?"

"Because then when he was asking me about giving Stoney a backstage pass, I thought how little I know about Stoney. I was so taken with him, but what if that was all part of his design? What if I gave a pass to the man who might be trying to kill Marty?"

Emily saw the tears well up in Tammy's eyes.

"I'm sure it's just a coincidence," Emily reassured her. "There's no reason to believe that Stoney is Cole McCay. If he was, why would he risk coming to the theater and possibly running into Marty? Marty's the only person who might recognize him."

Anna got Tammy a tissue, and Tammy dabbed at her eyes, trying not to smudge her heavy mascara.

"You didn't do anything wrong," Anna said. "Don't let that big goon make you feel bad. You do a wonderful job for him. You've given him half your life."

"Did you call Marty today?" Tammy asked Emily.

"No," Emily said. "I haven't been able to find that scrapbook, and I didn't feel like getting jumped on about it."

Tammy let out a little sob. "There's something else," she said. "I told Stoney about seeing the album." The tears ran down her cheeks.

"So what?" Anna said as she brought the box of tissue to the table.

Tammy blew her nose. "What if Stoney is Cole, and he came in here and stole that album so that no one would have a picture of him?"

Emily had a chilling image of a tall, dark man in her house, searching, taking what he wanted. She pictured the wide open back door and thought of the blood on the chisel.

"You're letting your imagination run wild," Anna soothed. "We figured out that Gordon must have taken it off somewhere with him to show to his buddies. They probably had a good laugh over it. Haven't you heard from Stoney yet?"

"No," Tammy said. "He seemed like such a nice guy, and he really acted as though he liked me." A fresh wave of tears assaulted her makeup. "But I called the Lakeshore Inn this morning, and they said they never had anyone registered there named Stoney Barnes."

The telephone rang and Emily went into the living room to answer it. When she returned to the kitchen, Tammy had stopped crying, and she and Anna were discussing who they could hire to finish the kitchen project.

They both stopped talking when they saw the look on Emily's face. Emily sat down at the table.

"That was the police," she said quietly. "They sent

the chisel I found under the coffee table in the living room last Friday to the crime lab. They asked me if Gordon had any tattoos.''

"Tattoos?" Anna said. "Why would they ask that? And how would we know?"

"Because they found human skin on the chisel. And the skin contained traces of tattoo ink."

Tammy looked from Emily's face to Anna's and cleared her throat. "Stoney has a tattoo," she said. She touched her shoulder.

Rocko rubbed against Emily's leg and let out a low yowl. Emily thought of the cat's strange behavior last Friday. "The police said they've checked with all Gordon's friends, and no one's seen him. They're coming over in a half hour to dust the house for fingerprints. This afternoon, they're going to organize a search of the woods. For his body."

"Oh, my God," Anna said softly. Tammy buried her face in her hands and started to cry again.

"He might have been killed right here," Anna said. "Maybe Gordon interrupted whoever was searching for the album."

The house suddenly seemed too quiet. Until now, Emily had believed that she was neither directly involved nor threatened in any way by Cole McCay and his dispute with Marty. Now she had to face the fact that someone may have broken into her home, maybe even committed murder within the walls where she had felt so safe and secure.

"We'd better go talk to Marty," Emily said. "We'll wait until the police are through. Then we'll go to the theater. Marty had better have Mr. Wells assign someone to watch our house too. And yours, Tammy."

Anna's face grew pale as the full implications of what Emily was saying came to her. Tammy's eyes grew wide. She didn't cry anymore.

The three women stayed at the kitchen table while two policemen went through the house, spreading ashy powder and taking prints from doors and doorknobs, windowsills, and the living room coffee table. Through the kitchen window, they could see another officer in the backyard, combing through the bushes and peering at the ground for footprints. As the men inside were finishing, the officer came in through the backdoor, holding a rag that was stained dark red.

"Ma'am," he said, showing the rag to Emily. "Do you know what's on this rag? I found it in the garage. Is this paint?"

"I don't know," Emily said. "Gordon had been staining our cabinets. It could be some stain he was mixing."

The officer dropped the rag into a plastic bag. "We'll have the lab identify it," he said.

Shortly after the police had left, after Emily had carefully checked to make certain all the windows and doors were securely locked, the three women walked into the Crystal Rose Theatre. From the office, Tammy called backstage and asked Marty to please come right upstairs.

"What'd he say?" Anna asked when she hung up the phone.

"He said he's busy, and he'll be up as soon as he can," Tammy said. "Do you want to go down there?" she asked Emily.

Emily thought of her last venture backstage to find Marty and decided that she'd just wait for him. Twenty minutes passed before Marty finally burst into the office, followed by a costumer and a stagehand both talking to him at the same time. He spent another five minutes giving them directions before they scurried off.

"What's going on?" he finally said, looking at the serious faces in front of him.

Emily told him what had happened. When she mentioned traces of tattoo ink found on the chisel, Marty's face lost its color.

"Cole McCay had a tattoo," he said. "On his wrist."

"Jesus," Tammy said, her voice rising toward hysteria. "Why didn't you tell that to Wells? Why didn't you tell us?"

"I didn't think of it before, okay?" Anger rose in his voice at her challenging tone.

"You've got to tell the police about Cole," Emily said. "How can they protect us and find him if they don't know who they're looking for? This isn't just about you anymore. Cole may have been in my house. He may have killed Gordon. If you don't tell the police, I will," she said.

"Goddammit, Emily, you can't do that," Marty shouted. "Is everybody out to ruin me?" He paced the room's length while Emily sat rigidly, her lips drawn into a tight line. Finally he came back to the desk and sat down across from them.

"I'm sorry I yelled at you, darlin'," he said to Emily. "I'm trying to put on a show here, and there's some psycho out there trying to drive me crazy."

Marty tilted his head to one side. His neck made a popping sound.

"Okay. Here's what we'll do," he said. "You realize that if word of this gets out, the first phone call I'll get tomorrow morning will be from TNN. They'll politely tell me that I'm a bad risk, and the TNN crew will politely leave my theater. Then the bank will politely put me in bankruptcy."

"We're talking about our lives being in danger, Marty," Emily said. "Don't you realize that?"

"Let me finish," Marty said. "You and Anna and Tammy come stay at the ranch tonight and tomorrow night. There's plenty of security out there now, and nobody will get in. And after the show Friday, we can all get back to normal.''

"How do you figure that?" Emily asked.

"Think about it," Marty said. "Think like a killer. If you've been in prison for thirty years, dreaming of the fame you might have had, what could you want more than a chance at the spotlight?" Marty brushed a speck of lint off his desk. "National TV, millions watching, the ultimate revenge."

Emily thought this over. If Cole had just wanted Marty dead, and if he'd been in town all week, he would have had plenty of chances to kill Marty.

"I want you to get Wells to put guards on our houses," Emily said. "Ours and Tammy's."

"That's ridiculous," Marty said. "I won't hear of it. The ranch has a fence and a gate and a twenty-thousand-dollar security system and a guard that patrols all night. What if Wells's guard falls asleep outside your house? Someone could pry any of those rickety old windows open with one hand or jimmy your antique locks with a credit card. You need to see about getting some work done on that house, Emily, once this is over."

"I'd planned on it, but I think someone may have murdered my handyman," Emily snapped. She didn't want to stay at Marty's. She didn't want to feel dependent. But what he said made sense. They had to take the situation seriously even though no outright threat had been made. And the ranch was a fortress compared to her house.

"All right," she said. "We'll stay out there until the show is over. Then we'll tell the police that they may be looking for Cole McCay. We don't have to go into all the details, and nothing that hurts your image may ever come out. We just want the police to find him."

"They won't find him," Marty said. "He'll find me."

*   *   *

When they got home from the theater, Emily and Anna packed a few things into overnight bags. More than once they startled each other as they moved around the house in the fading sunlight. Anna called to Emily several times from another room, just to reassure herself. She made sure Rocko had plenty of cat food and water, even though she knew she'd stop by the house tomorrow to check on him. She hated leaving him behind, but she knew that Marty disliked her pet and that Rocko would be more upset by the transition to new quarters than by her absence.

When they got out to Marty's house it was nearly dark, but the spotlights mounted around the closed gate illuminated the driveway. A uniformed guard came through a side door in the stone wall when they pulled up. He was a big, burly man, tall and stout with black hair showing under his Guardian cap. He leaned down and looked in at the two women, and Emily saw his eyes scan the backseat as well.

"I'm Emily Stone," she said. "This is my mother, Anna."

"I'm Joe Featherstone," the guard said. He didn't smile, but his tone was friendly. "Everything okay?"

"So far," Emily said.

"Go ahead," the guard said. He pushed the remote control he held in his hand, and the large gate rumbled to one side.

"This is like something out of a movie," Anna said, as Emily pulled through the gate.

"I'll be glad to see the happy ending," Emily said.

Inside, Linn made them as comfortable as they could be under the circumstances. Marty had called to say he wouldn't be home until past midnight, Linn said. Even though they had stopped for a sandwich on the way out to the ranch, Linn made coffee and presented an assortment of sweet rolls and small pastries. She showed them to adjoining guest rooms, freshly made up for their stay.

For a while, they watched the forty-six-inch television in Marty's den.

"This thing is giving me a headache," Anna declared, and went to bed at ten. An hour later, Emily was yawning, and she also retired. Putting her ear to the door that linked her room with her mother's, she could hear Anna's soft snore.

Emily was nearly asleep when she heard voices in the front hall. Tammy apparently had returned with Marty. She could hear their voices, but couldn't make out anything that was said except Marty calling good night to Tammy. Then there was a soft knock on her bedroom door. She thought of pretending to be asleep. Instead, she buttoned the top button on her cotton nightdress, and called for him to come in. He looked a wreck. He had dark shadows under his eyes. His shoulders sagged with fatigue. Even his usually perfect hair looked rumpled. He came over and sat down on the edge of the bed.

"You're a sight for sore eyes, baby," he said. "If this whole mess doesn't end soon, it's going to make an old man out of me."

Emily reached over to him and patted his shoulder. It would be so easy to offer him comfort. Part of her wanted to snuggle up with him and forget what was happening, and all that had led up to it. She wanted to be happy and to see the old easygoing Marty whom she thought she was beginning to love not so long ago. Marty slid closer to her and wrapped her in his arms and kissed her cheek. When she shut her eyes and smelled his familiar scent, she almost gave in, almost pulled him down with her onto the bed. It would feel so good to fall asleep with her head on his wide shoulder.

Emily's reverie ended when she felt Marty's kiss subtly change, his lips pressing harder, his hands starting to roam across her back. He kissed her neck, working his way down toward her shoulders and began making little noises of appreciation.

"Stop," Emily said. He didn't.

She squirmed to release herself from his embrace.

"It'll be so good, baby," he whispered while he wound his fingers into her hair. "I need you so much."

Emily reached for his hair and pulled on it hard, drawing his face back from her neck. "Stop it, Marty," she said. She was whispering, but he heard her clearly. "Stop. I don't want to do this tonight," she said, releasing her hold on his hair.

He let her go and leaned back, but he stroked her cheek and the lace at the top of her nightgown. "What's the matter, honey?" he asked. "We've been waiting for this for so long. I don't want to wait anymore."

"My mother's sleeping right on the other side of that door," Emily whispered.

"Well, let's make sure it's locked," Marty said. His playful attitude in the face of her distress deepened her resolve.

"I don't want to discuss this," she said in a low voice. "I'm just telling you that I want you to go now."

"Why don't you come back to my room?" he asked. "It's clear on the other side of the house. It'll be like sneaking out when you were a teenager."

"Read my lips," she said slowly. "I don't want to make love with you tonight."

Finally, Marty looked hurt. He pulled away from her a bit, but didn't get up off the bed. He studied his hands.

"I'm sorry I've been so hard to get along with these last couple of days," he said. "You've found out about a lot of dirt in my past, and I wouldn't blame you if you didn't love me anymore." He shot a glance at her. Emily's expression didn't change. He took her hand and smoothed it as though he were applying lotion. "All I'd ask is that you just try to be patient with this old boy and give me another chance once this storm's over. You'll let me come in out of the rain, won't you?''

His melodramatic pitch didn't sway Emily.

"Let's just get through this," she said. "By next week, this will all be in the past."

"You know how much I love you?" Marty said, his eyes pleading like a begging dog.

Emily avoided the question.

"Let's just get some sleep tonight. Okay?" She gave his arm another pat, but this time it was dismissive and decidedly unpassionate. "You need some rest, and so do I."

Marty sighed and rubbed his face.

"You're right, angel," he said. He grinned at her as though he didn't have a care in the world, as though there wasn't a guard outside watching for a killer. "You get your beauty rest, not that you need it." He stood up and headed for the door. "See you in the morning," he said without looking back as he pulled the door shut behind him.

Emily waited until she could no longer hear his steps padding along the carpeted hallway. Then she got up and went to the door and peeked out. There was no one in sight, and the house was silent. She closed the door, locked it from the inside, and got in bed. For a minute she considered whether she should have accepted his offer of love. She could imagine him being a tender and attentive lover, but as she thought the act through to its conclusion, she imagined Marty hopping out of bed when he had finished, giving her a pat, and saying "have a nice day" as he breezed out of the room. The thought left her with an empty feeling in the pit of her stomach. She reached over and turned off the nightstand lamp.

On the shoulder of Lake Road 212, across the cove from Marty's house, a man sat in the dark in a faded black pickup. He leaned back and took a swig from a pint of Jim Beam. He smoked a small cigar and hummed quietly to himself. At midnight, he saw Emily's light go off.

✷ CHAPTER 18 ✷

Emily slept fitfully. On Thursday morning, she met a haggard Anna at the breakfast nook in Marty's kitchen. Linn, of course, had coffee and breakfast ready for them. Marty and Tammy had left already for the theater where Emily knew full-scale dress rehearsals would go on all day and into the evening.

"I don't know if I can take another night in that bed," Anna groaned, stretching her back. "It's hard as a rock."

Emily also was eager for the stay at the ranch to end. She didn't look forward to a repeat performance of the bedroom scene the night before.

When they had dressed, Emily dropped Anna off at the home of her friend Anita Hanson. The two had a downtown beautification project they were working on, and Anna assured Emily that Anita would be happy to deliver her back to Marty's that afternoon. "She'll love getting a look at that place," Anna said.

Emily drove up to her house and pushed the garage door opener, but she left the car in the driveway. There was no reason to think anyone might be there, but Emily took every step with caution, watching for movements in the shadows and listening for any sound. In the kitchen, Rocko greeted her with loud meows and did a little cat

dance to show he was glad to see her. The house was
quiet as a tomb, and Emily hurried to replenish the cat's
food and gather the clothing she and Anna would need
for the night. They would come back together on Friday
afternoon to dress for the show. Marty had said he'd send
a guard with them.

Emily locked the empty house behind her, relieved to
get into her car after first checking to be certain no one
had hidden in the backseat while she was inside. Then
she had a few errands to do. She stopped at the mall and
picked up a new pair of pantyhose and some shoe polish,
and bought a necklace with red and blue beads. It would
look festive with the white cotton dress she planned to
wear to the show tomorrow. Marty hadn't sent anyone
from a dress shop over with new clothes for her on this
occasion.

She kept her one o'clock appointment to have her hair
trimmed. The beautician, knowing that Emily was dating
Marty, was full of questions about the Fourth of July
special, but Emily didn't encourage her conversation. After awhile, the beautician took the hint and fell silent. By
four o'clock, Emily had nothing else to do. She didn't
want to go back to the ranch. There would be nothing to
do there, either. A little concerned about Tammy's state
of mind, she decided to stop by the theater. Marty would
probably be too busy to notice her, and Tammy might
need the moral support.

Emily went in through the lobby and saw it was bustling with people buying tickets for tomorrow's show.
She watched the crowd for a moment, trying to spot the
Guardian Security people, but if they were there, they
were certainly unobtrusive. The activity in the lobby gave
Emily a good feeling. Maybe everything would blow
over, and life would soon be back to normal. Still reticent
to go backstage, Emily called Marty's office from the
lobby phone.

"Tammy, it's Emily. I'm in the lobby. How's everything going?"

"Complete chaos," Tammy said. She sounded tired.

"Do you want to take a break and come down and have a cup of coffee?" Emily asked.

"Love to," Tammy said.

When Tammy came into the Faded Rose, Emily was shocked at how worn out she looked.

"Didn't you sleep last night?"

"Barely," Tammy said. "I'm used to my waterbed. I can't wait to get home when all this cloak-and-dagger stuff ends. I wish Marty would just tell the cops everything. Maybe they'd be able to find Cole then."

"Any word from Stoney?"

"Of course not," Tammy said. "I feel like a complete fool. I wish I would have found out more about him."

"It sounded to me like you quizzed him pretty thoroughly that night at Dante's," Emily said.

"And that's another thing," Tammy said, twirling one of her curls nervously. "That was the night that old guy was mugged in the restroom there. When Stoney went to pay the bill, he was gone for an awfully long time. Could he have gone into the john and rolled someone with me sitting right out there waiting for him?"

"Why would you think Stoney did that?"

"Because what if he is Cole McCay?" Tammy said, lowering her voice. "If he just got out of prison, he certainly wouldn't have had money to spend on a dinner like that. Add it up. He's from Georgia. He's got a tattoo. He says he's a friend of Marty's, but he never comes by to see him. And he cozies up to Marty's assistant and hands himself a backstage pass. I'd like to get my hands on the son-of-a-bitch."

Emily was glad to see Tammy showing some spirit again.

"It's too bad you never got a look at his car," Emily said.

"Yeah," Tammy said. "That could have been carefully calculated on his part, too. And that could have been why he didn't invite me into his room at the Lakeshore Inn. He didn't even have a room there. He was probably sleeping under a bridge."

"Maybe he was staying at the inn, but the clerk you called didn't find his name in the records," Emily said. "It could have just been an oversight. Maybe you should try calling again."

Tammy stared at Emily with a hint of hope in her eyes. "You think so?" she asked. "Maybe you're right. Maybe he's just been busy with business and that's why he hasn't called. I'd give anything if that were true."

"Well, why don't you call the inn again?"

Tammy thought it over. "Better yet," she said. "Why don't we get out of here for a while and ride over there. Marty won't even notice I'm not around, I'm sure. I'll talk to the desk clerk and tell him I need to deliver something to Stoney. Maybe if I describe him, they'll know who I'm talking about."

The prospect of finding out that she hadn't been made the fool seemed to give Tammy a new burst of energy. Emily liked the idea of getting out of the theater, so she agreed to drive Tammy to the inn.

"If Stoney's not there, let's go up to the Brass Rail and talk to the bartender. Maybe he'll know something about him," Tammy suggested as they drove toward the lake.

"Playing Nancy Drew now, are we?" Emily said.

Tammy looked at her blankly, and Emily realized that somehow Tammy had grown up without reading the series that Emily had loved so much as a child.

"She was a girl detective," Emily explained.

"I'm not playing detective," Tammy said, touching

her shoulder. "I'd just like to get a look at Stoney's wrist to see if there's a big cut in his tattoo. Don't forget, I'm marked for life because of that creep."

The desk clerk at the inn was polite, but after looking back through the sign-in sheets and checking reservations and credit card receipts, he found no record of a Stoney Barnes. Tammy's description of Stoney didn't help either. The desk clerk said he couldn't remember anyone who looked like that.

"Mostly we get retired couples here," he said. "Businessmen usually stay up at the Holiday Inn or one of the chains."

"Stop at the Brass Rail," Tammy said. "Might as well try while we're close by. Besides, I'd like a cold beer."

When they each had a Bud Light, Tammy asked the bartender if he remembered seeing her in there the week before with a good looking guy. The bartender said he didn't. Tammy described Stoney in detail—the dark suit he had worn, his hair, his demeanor—but nothing rang a bell with the bartender.

"He had a tattoo of a dagger on his wrist," Tammy said as a last resort.

"Oh, yeah," the bartender said, brightening. "I do remember a guy with a tattoo like that. But he wasn't any slick dresser when I saw him. He looked like a bum. I commented on the tattoo, but he was kind of nasty about it. Pulled his sleeve down like he didn't want me to see it. I only saw him that one time, though. He came in to pay his rent."

"What?" Tammy asked. "His rent?"

"Yeah," the bartender said. "The cook's got a little dump of a trailer north of town he rents out. I guess this guy had seen the ad in the paper."

"Is the cook here?" asked Emily, her reporter's instinct springing to life.

The cook was a big man who looked like he loved to eat.

"Barnes?" he said. "That's not the name he gave me. Said his name was Doug Brown. He had cash for the rent, so I gave him directions and the key to the place. It's just an old run-down trailer that was sitting on the property when I bought it. As bad as people need cheap housing around here, I figured I'd try to rent it. I drove out by it a couple of days ago and saw a black pickup parked there, but I didn't go inside. I figured the worst he could do would be trash it up with beer bottles, or maybe set it on fire, which wouldn't be bad," the cook chortled. "Save me having to have it hauled off some-day."

"We need to get in touch with him," Tammy said. "Can you give us directions to it?"

"Sure," he said. "But if I were going out there, I might take a man along. This guy looked like he could be kind of a rough character."

He drew the women a map. The trailer was on a dirt road about six miles outside city limits. There was a pawnshop on the highway at the turnoff.

"Let's go," said Tammy when they got back in the car.

"Go there?" Emily said. "I don't want to go out there. What if it *is* Cole? Let's call the police."

"And tell them what? We don't know if it's Cole. What if it's really Stoney?"

"Why would he be living in a trailer if he's who he said he was? And where did he get the money to pay for those dinners if he's staying in a cheap trailer?" Emily asked.

"Maybe he spent his last dime on me," Tammy said, still clinging to the hope that she hadn't been taken in. "What if he really is an old friend of Marty's who's just down on his luck and was counting on Marty to help him out? If that's the case, and we call the cops on him, Marty will be even more angry with me. Let's just drive up there and look and see if the black truck is there. Besides, it might not even be Stoney. There are probably a lot of guys with tattoos around here.''

"I think it's a bad idea," Emily argued.

A gleam came into Tammy's eyes. "So what if it is Cole, and we find him? Marty will be forever in our debt.''

This idea had some appeal to Emily, who finally agreed it wouldn't hurt just to drive out there and take a look. They drove north and turned left onto a narrow graveled road beside a rundown pawnshop. A crooked ''Closed'' sign hung in the front window. A half mile later, the road forked and they followed it to the left. Three-quarters of a mile farther, they saw a small trailer set back from the road. Rust crept up the sides of the faded box. The front yard was overgrown with weeds. A dirt driveway led up to a small, rickety porch.

"Go slow," Tammy whispered.

There were no cars in sight, and no sign of life around the building. "Want to pretend you're with the Welcome Wagon and go knock on the door?''

"No," Tammy said seriously. "Drive on by.''

Emily drove past the trailer a hundred yards and turned off the road, following a tractor path in the adjacent pasture. Through the trees, the trailer was still visible. A trail through waist-high weeds led to the back door.

Emily stopped. "Now what?" she asked Tammy. "Whoever was there is long gone.''

Tammy rolled down her window and listened. Then she opened the car door. "I'm going to take a look.''

"You're crazy!" Emily said. "You're not going near that place. What if he's got a pit bull in the backyard?''

"There wasn't any dog there," Tammy said. "There's no car. There's no one there. I'll just go peak inside. You stay in the car with the motor running. If someone's in there, or someone drives up in front, I'll just run back to the car.''

Emily shook her head. "This is not a good idea.''

"I'll be right back," Tammy said.

Emily grabbed her arm. "What if Stoney's in there? He'll think you were checking up on him and that'll be the end of your love life.''

"I'll tell him I was worried about him, and that the bartender told me how to find him," Tammy said.

"And if he's really Cole?''

"Stoney-Cole, Cole-Stoney," Tammy chanted bitterly. She got out of the car and shut the door. She bent down to look in the window. "Emily, I've got to find out.''

In the gloom of the overhanging cedar trees, Tammy walked quickly up the path to the trailer. There was no sound other than the purr of the car idling and the occasional snap of a twig under her foot. With a growing sense of foreboding, Tammy mounted the two narrow wooden steps leading to the trailer's back door. No sound came from inside. Tammy peered in through the small screened window in the door, cupping her hands for a clearer view. Somewhere in the woods, a crow squawked.

Tammy turned back and motioned for Emily to join her. Emily turned off the ignition.

"There's no one here," Tammy called. "Come look at this.''

Emily got out of the car, gripping the car keys in her fist with one key sticking from between her fingers in what she realized was a woefully inadequate form of self-defense. This would be a lousy weapon against a butcher knife, she thought. Tammy stepped off the stairs to make room for Emily, who also pressed her hands and face to the window. She could see into the tiny living area where a card table and a folding chair sat in the middle of the room. Several crushed beer cans and a half-empty whiskey bottle rested beside an empty glass on the table. Beside the front door, she could see another small table holding a messy pile of newspapers. She couldn't see anything to indicate that the trailer had been recently occupied.

"What am I supposed to see?" she whispered.

"Look at the wall beside the door."

Emily pressed closer to the window. Thumbtacked on the living room wall beside the front door, directly across from her, was an eight-by-ten glossy of Marty Rose.

Emily backed down the steps away from the door and grabbed Tammy's arm, pulling her toward the car.

"Let's get out of here," she said.

"No, wait," Tammy said, slipping her grasp and going up the stairs again. She tried the doorknob. To Emily's dismay, the door swung open as though an invisible host had been waiting for them.

Tammy looked at Emily, then stepped into the trailer.

Emily thought of running for the car. But she couldn't leave Tammy alone.

"Tammy," she called softly.

Tammy came to the door. "No one's here," she said in a normal tone of voice. "You'd better come take a look." She disappeared back into the trailer.

Cautiously looking over her shoulders at the woods, Emily went inside. Tammy was standing in the living room.

"Look," she said, pointing to the back wall of the room. The air was hot and stale, and there was a heavy, sweet odor that reminded Emily of the rotting rose. She turned and looked where Tammy was pointing. The back wall of the living room was covered with pictures of Marty Rose. There must have been forty or fifty pictures thumbtacked or taped to the wall. They were pictures from the scrapbook. There was the young Marty, the young Chick and Nita, staring at her. And in the center, set off by extra space, was a yellowed picture of the Cadillac Cowboys: Chick, Marty, and a dark-haired boy that Emily had never seen.

"It's Stoney," Tammy said. "He hasn't changed much in thirty years."

"Let's get out of here," Emily said, heading for the open door.

"Wait," Tammy said, moving into the small kitchen. "Here's the backstage pass." She picked up the laminated tag that hung from a nylon cord. "That slimebag," she said through gritted teeth. "I'd like to cram this down his lying goddamn throat."

"Let's go," Emily said urgently. "Come on."

"What a pig," Tammy said, surveying the dirty dishes piled in the sink and the remnants of sandwich crusts and fast food. She went to the small, grubby refrigerator and opened it.

"What are you doing?" Emily asked in disbelief. "He could come back any second."

"Let him," Tammy said in a threatening tone. She slammed the refrigerator door and walked into the doorway of the tiny bedroom. Tammy wound the nylon cord of the backstage pass around her fist. "I'd like to show him my new tattoo." She looked into the bedroom. "Oh, this is very nice." She pointed at something and looked toward Emily. Emily scurried to stand beside Tammy in the bedroom doorway. "There's his Stoney suit," Tammy said. Hanging on a hook on the bedroom wall was a meticulously pressed dark suit, complete with white shirt, red tie and a spiffy red handkerchief peeking from one pocket. That's when they heard the truck pull up.

Before they could move, the truck door slammed and footsteps banged across the front porch. Emily glanced at the back door which had swung closed. She saw the front door begin to open. She pushed Tammy into the bedroom toward a closet covered by a tattered curtain. Emily ducked into the closet, pulling Tammy behind her. The closet was about four feet wide. The only thing inside was a large, square, dark green plastic garment bag hanging from the rod by three hooks. They pushed past the garment bag and froze against the closet's back wall. In front of them, the curtain swung for a moment then was still. They clung to each other, and Emily put her hand against Tammy's mouth. They held their breath.

As Cole shut the trailer's front door, the back door slowly swung open a few inches. Cole glanced around the trailer as he walked to the back door. He opened it and looked outside, then closed the door and tossed a folded newspaper on the card table. Then he went to the refrigerator and took out a beer. He unscrewed the cap, tossed it in the direction of the kitchen counter, took a long swig, and sat down at the card table. Cole propped his feet up on the card table and opened the newspaper. He wore dusty work books, faded blue jeans, torn above one knee, and a rumpled, long-sleeved plaid shirt with plastic pearl buttons. The stubble of several days' beard growth made his face look narrow and pointed. He put the newspaper on the table and took another pull on his beer, unsnapped the wrists of his shirt sleeves, and rolled them up to the elbow. On his left wrist was a dirty white bandage. He hummed to himself as he got up and went into the kitchen, rummaging through a pile of crumpled Burger King bags on the kitchen counter.

In the closet, Emily tried to slow her heart rate. Tammy was frozen still, her eyes wide as saucers. Not so eager to get even with her lover boy now, Emily thought. What a pair of fools. We'll be lucky to get out of this alive. She wished she had told Tammy the gory details of why Cole had been in prison. Maybe if she'd known, she wouldn't have been so eager to go into the trailer.

Outside, the sun was going down. Cole switched on

the kitchen light. Emily could see him through a small tear in the closet's curtain. She watched him shuffle through the trash on the counter and pick up a six-inch-long ebony-handled knife. Cole pushed a button and the switchblade sprung out.

"Let's see how we're doing here," Cole said. His low voice sounded amplified in the tiny trailer, and Emily felt Tammy shiver. She squeezed Tammy's hand, warning her to be silent.

Emily watched Cole slit the edge of the gauze with the knife and unwrap it from his wrist. He let the gauze fall onto the floor and set the knife on the counter. Emily could see the blade gleam in the reflected light from the bare bulb.

"Looking good," Cole said, examining black stitches that crisscrossed his tattoo. Among the burger bags lay a spool of black darning thread. A long, curved needle protruded from the top of the spool. "Nice work, doc," Cole said to himself as he delicately fingered the wound. He pulled at one of the stitches, then winced. "Damn," he said.

Cole went to the refrigerator and took out a half-empty bread bag and an open package of pickle loaf. The meat was dried along one edge and Cole peeled off a chunk, letting it drop to the floor. He put several pieces of the meat between two slices of bread, carried the sandwich back to the table, and continued to look through the newspaper. Emily could hear him turning the pages.

"Let's get out of here," Tammy whispered almost soundlessly. Emily squeezed her arm hard. She put her mouth close to Tammy's ear.

"He's got a knife," she whispered. Tammy closed her eyes.

Cole finished the sandwich and went over to the end table by the front door. He found a tape and carried it to a small cassette player on the card table. A few moments later, the two women heard Marty Rose begin to sing. Accompanying Marty's rugged voice was a harmony neither of them had ever heard. It was a stunningly beautiful voice, deep and soft and rich. His singing was as smooth and steady as Perry Como, as rich and deep as Pavarotti. The southern accent was a gentle touch. Cole was singing his song. His pacing and inflection didn't quite match Marty's and on some phrases, the two voices clashed. It made Marty sound like he was offkey. "Two Hearts Tied" ended, but Cole's voice continued with another verse:

> *You stole my song. You done me wrong.*
> *And when you've died, I'll laugh inside.*
> *The world will know 'bout two hearts tied.*

"Sounding good," Cole told himself, shutting off the cassette. "Rose never could sing."

Emily saw him come into view walking toward the bedroom, and she went rigid. Cole stopped by the suit that hung from the peg and brushed at it with a small wisk broom. "Got to look good in the spotlights," he said. He laid the broom on on nightstand and picked up a deck of cards.

"Haan-dy-man. Oh, haan-dy-man," he called in a low drawl. "Where are you, handyman? Got time for a game of solitaire, Mr. Handyman?" He stood by the foot of the bed and shuffled the cards. "You've been losing a lot lately, but I'll give you one last chance to make it up. This is our last night together, you know."

Cole came to the closet and slid the curtain halfway aside. Emily and Tammy shrank deeper into the shadows. Cole unzipped the garment bag.

"Come out, come out," he taunted.

As the garment bag's sides fell loose, the women saw Gordon, lashed to the hooks by a rope wound under his

arms. His head tilted back, mouth gaping, and his thick
purplish tongue showed between his teeth. His eyes pro
truded like marbles. Tammy was face to face with Gor
don. Her scream vibrated the tin walls of the trailer. With
strength born of terror, she tore through the curtain, slam
ming the startled Cole against the bedroom wall. With a
growl of fury, he dashed after her, catching her as she
was halfway through the trailer's back door. He grabbed
her by her hair, got his hand around her throat and shook
her. He picked her up and threw her like a rag doll of
the steps. Tammy landed on her back and scrambled to
gain her feet, but Cole was on her. He backhanded her
with his right hand and she reeled back, falling onto the
path.

Behind Cole, Emily raised the whiskey bottle and
swung it at Cole's head with all her strength. Stunned
senseless, he dropped to his knees. Emily dragged
Tammy to her feet, and they stumbled toward the car
She shoved Tammy into the car and as she opened the
driver's-side door, she saw Cole coming up the path. In
the dim light from the trailer, she could see the switch
blade.

She jammed the key into the ignition. The car started
immediately and for a fleeting moment, she thought they
would make it. But Cole was there. He grabbed Tammy
by the hair through the open window and held the knife
to her throat.

"Turn off the engine, hold the keys where I can see
them, and get out of the car, real slow," he told Emily.

As Emily complied, Cole yanked Tammy's door open
and pulled her out. With the knife again at her throat, he
made Emily lead the way back to the trailer. Inside, Cole
slammed Tammy's head against the wall. She crumpled
to the dirty carpeting. He turned and in an instant had
Emily pinned to the floor, straddling her chest and hold
ing the knife over her face.

"So, it's Marty's girl come to visit. You smacked me a good one, you little bitch," he said, rubbing the back of his head.

Emily was overwhelmed with horror. This was the man who, in the same position, had sliced up a young woman. She could see his lips moving, but she didn't know what he was saying. It was as though she were out of her body, looking down and seeing herself and Cole from the top of the silo in her nightmare. But this nightmare was real. Cole stood up then, and Emily could see him motioning with the knife for her to get up. She lifted on one elbow and shook her head, trying to regain herself. She heard Cole call toward the bedroom. "Wake up, handyman. We got dates."

☆ CHAPTER 19 ☆

Cole went to the kitchen. Emily sat up and inched toward Tammy who was sprawled on her side, moaning. Her right cheek was flaming red and the area around her eye was beginning to swell. Emily pulled on Tammy, urging her to sit up.

"That's good," Cole said when he turned and saw them. "You make her shut up or I will." He brandished a black pistol in one hand and the switchblade in the other. He sat down on the folding chair facing them.

"Well, if it isn't my little girfriend Tammy," he said, grinning. "You come to find ol' Stoney? Still want me to make love to you?" His chuckle sent a chill through Emily.

Cole laid the pistol on the card table and transferred the knife to his right hand. He leaned toward the women, resting his elbows on his knees and staring at Emily through narrowed eyes.

"I was planning on going to the show tomorrow," he said. "I've got a date with your boyfriend, but you little ladies have kind of screwed up my plans now."

"Well, we'll just leave and you can—" Emily began.

Cole took two steps and crouched beside Emily, holding the knife's tip against her cheek.

"Shut up," he said. "Lie down on the floor on your stomachs. Now!" he shouted in Emily's face.

They both did as they were told. The rug smelled of diesel oil and old urine. Emily could see a dead cockroach an inch from her nose. Three feet away, Tammy's face was contorted with fear.

"People are expecting us," Emily said. "They know where we are."

"I don't think I believe you," Cole said after a moment. "I think if anyone had known what you were up to, you two wouldn't be out here alone. But since you decided to be nosey, I guess I've got the winning hand. I was just planning to waltz on into the theater tomorrow—backstage, thanks to sweet Tammy—and surprise my old friend. I was going to blow his goddamn brains out on national TV But now you two are going to be missing, and Tammy won't be there to get me into position. That plan ain't got a chance in hell of working."

He walked over to stand between the women and placed his boot in the center of Tammy's back. Cole leaned on her, jiggling her body, and Tammy groaned.

"Leave her alone," Emily said. His kick to her side knocked the breath out of her in a great rush and sent pain shooting through her ribs.

"You will speak when I tell you to," Cole said, crouching between them. He grabbed a handful of Emily's hair and cut it off with a quick flick of his knife. He slapped the hank of hair at Emily's face and then Tammy's. "You will do what I say," he chanted as he slapped with the hair. "You will obey me." He dropped the hair between them and held the tip of the knife to Tammy's temple. Emily could see Tammy trembling.

"Do you know who I am?" He was looking at Emily.

"Yes," Emily said.

"Did Marty tell you about me?"

"Yes."

"Did he tell you about Devil's Ridge?" Cole's voice was low like someone talking in the back of church.

Emily didn't know what to say. She saw the tip of the knife press deeper into the skin of Tammy's vulnerable temple.

"Yes," she said.

"Then you know that I haven't been having much fun for the last thirty years, and you know I've got a score to settle."

Cole stood up. He paced slowly around them in a circle for what seemed like an eternity.

"We're going to go see Marty," Cole said. "Where's he at right now?"

"He's at the theater," Emily said, thinking of the guards and the throng of people who might mean safety.

"Too many people there," Cole said. "We'll go out to his house, and you'll call him and get him to come home."

Emily thought of her mother and Linn alone in the house. If Cole somehow got past the guard at the gate, her mother would be in grave danger.

"He's got guards at the house," Emily said. "He thought you might come here. He's got a guard at the gate and one in the house. He's got surveillance cameras and an alarm. You'll never get in there."

Cole paced around them again.

"I'll get in there," he said. "And we won't go to the house. My guess is there's no guard on that swanky houseboat."

He knelt and held the knife against Tammy's temple again. He ran the knife toward her chin and a thin line of blood appeared. Tammy moaned and Emily could see tears squeezing out from between the slits of her eyelids. "How about it? Guards on the houseboat?"

"No," Emily said. "There's no guard there." Emily knew where Marty hid the keys to the boat in the barbecue grill on the deck. If she got Cole onto the boat, at least her mother and Linn wouldn't be in any danger.

Cole kicked Tammy in the ribs.

"Sit up," he bellowed to them.

Emily sat up. She hurt all over. Tammy hadn't moved, so Emily pulled on her arm. "Sit up," she told Tammy. "Do what he says."

Cole picked up a small electric fan from the corner of the room and cut off the cord with his knife. He pulled Tammy's hands behind her back and wrapped the cord tightly around her wrists.

"Now, Mrs. Emily Rose, I've got a little job for you," Cole said. "You go in the bedroom and get that pretty suit of mine."

When Emily was in the bedroom, she couldn't help but look at Gordon once more. Poor Gordon, she thought. I may be joining you soon.

When Emily returned with the suit, Cole was standing in the middle of the room wearing nothing but his briefs. Emily felt her knees buckle. Cole was holding a pair of cowboy boots. He threw them at Emily's feet, and she could see the embossed pattern of a rose.

"Dress me," he said.

Emily didn't move.

"Come on, now," Cole said. "All the big stars have dressers. I'm sure Marty's got a few of them."

Cole directed her every move with great delight. Emily's fear was replaced with utter humiliation.

"Careful with that zipper," Cole chuckled.

When Emily had finished, Cole picked up his cowboy hat, and placed it on his head with great care. He looked in the hazy wall mirror beside the scrapbook photos and cocked the hat slightly. Then he held out his hands.

"It's showtime," he said.

"What are you going to do?" Emily asked.

"Cash in my tickets," he said. He pointed at Emily.

"Ticket one." Then at Tammy. "Ticket two." Cole tore a piece of duct tape from the cracked living room window and wrapped it over Tammy's mouth.

He took a quick look around the trailer, as though forgetting something. He snapped his fingers and went to the refrigerator where he took out one beautiful long-stemmed red rose.

"Let's go," he said as he poked at Tammy with the toe of his polished boot.

Cole held the gun on the two women as they made their way across the field to her car. Tammy was dazed and silent, but the cool night air cleared Emily's head a little. When they reached the car, Cole told Emily to open the trunk.

"The trunk? Why the trunk?" she asked.

"Good God Almighty, woman. Do exactly what I say or I'll kill you both right here, right now."

Emily didn't hesitate. Cole grabbed Tammy by the front of her blouse and shoved her into the trunk.

"Please, Cole," Emily implored. "It's too hot in there. She'll suffocate."

Cole turned to Emily. "I thought I told you to shut up. The sun's down. She'll be all right. Besides, she needs to sweat off some of those fancy meals I bought her. Or should I say the meals some fat tub-of-guts tourist bought her."

Cole leaned over and smoothed the tape over Tammy's mouth.

"If you make one little noise, I'll kill your girlfriend. Then I'll run this car into the lake with you right where you lay."

Tammy looked up at the man with whom she thought she had been falling in love. He had deceived her, abused her, and now he was probably going to kill her. All she felt was rage. When Cole saw it in her eyes, he did a double take, gave a little chuckle, and slammed the trunk shut.

On the way to the house, Cole went over what Emily was to say, but all Emily could think of was getting Tammy out of the trunk.

"Slow down, goddammit," Cole barked. "I've been waiting thirty years for this. We'll get there soon enough."

As they pulled up to the front gate, big Joe walked up to the car.

"Hi, Joe," Emily said with a smile. "This is Stoney Barnes. We're meeting Marty at the boat. He'll be here soon, but don't tell him Stoney's here. It's a surprise, okay? They went to high school together."

Joe took a careful look at Stoney.

"No offense, ma'am," he said, "but no one I don't know goes in without authorization from Mr. Rose. Those are the rules."

"Oh, please, Joe?" Emily asked. "Marty's been working so hard. He needs this diversion. Can't I authorize it this one time?"

Joe stood up straight and put one hand on his waist and the other on his holstered pistol. It wasn't a threat, but a show of authority. He seemed about to repeat that he couldn't break protocol when Cole spoke up.

"That's okay, sir," he said in his smooth drawl. "I understand. Emily's filled me in on the whole darned mess. It's a shame the dirt one disgruntled employee can kick up. It's just that we were best friends back in Wimberley, Texas, where we grew up, and I wanted to surprise Marty before the big show."

Joe didn't move.

Cole reached into his breast pocket. "Here," he said, holding something towards Joe. "Look at this."

Emily looked down at the snapshot Cole was holding out. It was the three Cadillac Cowboys.

Joe reached down and took the picture. He recognized Marty and the passenger in the car. He grinned.

"My, my, my," Joe said. "You boys grew some sideburns back then, didn't you." He handed the photo back to Cole.

"Yeah," Cole said wistfully. "We were some cool cats in those days."

Joe leaned over and looked in the window. He shook his head a little.

"Okay, Miss Stone," Joe said. "Y'all go ahead. But, listen. No more surprises, okay?"

"I promise," Emily said, thinking of Tammy in the trunk. "No more surprises."

As they entered the gate, Cole stared straight ahead. "That dumb Indian was about five seconds from getting his head blown off."

"That would have been real smart." The words were out of her mouth before she could stop herself.

Cole looked at her.

"You would have been next."

★ CHAPTER 20 ★

As Emily drove toward the dock, she could see the brightly lit house. She was certain Anna was there by now. She stopped in front of the dock and without waiting for instructions, popped the trunk release with a lever under the seat. Cole glared at her.

Sweat poured down Tammy's battered face, but Emily could tell by her narrowed eyes and the set of her mouth that Tammy was all right. Cole pulled her out of the trunk.

"Get on the boat," he said, pointing the pistol. "Don't make a sound."

Cole tried the sliding glass doors of the houseboat. He turned to Emily. She expected him to force her to tell him where the key was. Instead, he grinned, went to the barbecue grill, and extracted the key.

"Cole McCay's nobody's fool," he hissed as he unlocked the cabin. "I had my own little private party out here the night ol' Marty was celebrating his birthday. Had me a little tour of the house, too. Nice party. Too bad I wasn't invited."

In the houseboat's front room, Cole pushed Tammy onto one of the couches and told Emily to sit down beside her. He ripped the tape off Tammy's mouth.

"No need to worry about that little mustache you were getting anymore," he said.

He turned on the small map light above the captain's wheel and sat in the elevated chair. From a compartment next to the wheel, Cole pulled out a map of Table Rock Lake and spread it out on the console. He traced a path with his finger. "Nice," he muttered. He put the boat's key in the ignition and turned it a half turn, lighting up the boat's gauges. "And a full tank of gas too. Perfect."

Cole stood up and picked up a cellular phone that hung in its cradle beside the kitchen counter. He handed the phone to Emily, sat down beside Tammy, and put the knife to her throat. "Call your boyfriend," he said. "Tell him to come right home."

"He's going to know something's wrong if I tell him to come out to the boat," Emily said.

"Make sure he doesn't," Cole said. "Tell him you want a little romance on the lake tonight. Tell him you've got champagne, and you're naked. If Marty's still as hot for the girls as he used to be, he'll be here quick as a jack rabbit."

Emily's stomach twisted with another wave of fear. There was no doubt in her mind that Cole intended to kill all of them, and Emily saw little chance of rescue. Marty was their only hope. Emily dialed the stage manager's cellphone number. When he answered on the second ring, Emily identified herself and told him she needed to talk to Marty immediately.

"He's just going over some last-minute notes," the stage manager said. "Can he call you back?"

"No," Emily said. "I have to talk to him right now. Get him."

As she waited, Emily could hear stagehands shouting and an occasional burst from a horn or guitar. When Marty answered the phone, he sounded annoyed.

"I'm almost finished," he said. "What do you need?"

"I need you," Emily said, trying to sound sexy. "I've got champagne on ice, and I'm waiting for you." She paused. "I'm wearing a little black silk teddy I bought today just for the occasion."

"Are you?" Suddenly Marty sounded interested. "Why the change of heart? You weren't too friendly last night."

"I've been thinking about you all day, and I think we should be close tonight. For good luck. How soon can you be here?"

"About a half hour," Marty said. "Can you wait that long?"

"I'm not sure," Emily said, trying to sound passionate. "I've been waiting a long time. Can you hurry?"

"I'll fly," Marty said.

"Marty?" Emily said. "I'm out on the boat. I don't want my mother to know. It'll be secret this way."

"You sexy angel, you," Marty said. "The captain will be there in twenty minutes. Keep the champagne cold and your body hot." He hung up.

"He'll be here in twenty minutes," Emily said, handing the phone back to Cole.

"Good," Cole said, a sneer curling his upper lip. "You did that just right. I bet old Marty's drooling over that little black teddy right now. He hasn't changed a bit, has he? He never did care who it was as long as he could get what he wanted when he wanted it."

Cole opened the small refrigerator and took out a bottle of beer. "That was real nice of someone to restock," he said. "I drank what was in here during the birthday party."

He stood in front of Emily. He took the pistol out of the pocket of his suit jacket and ran the tip of the barrel around her chin and down one side of her neck. As Emily looked up at him, she could see a bead of perspiration form on his upper lip.

"I'd like to see you in that black teddy myself," Cole said. "You sure looked pretty climbing that ladder in your garage the day I put your handyman to rest." Cole moved the tip of the gun along the collar of her blouse, stopping at the top button.

"You didn't know I was watching you then, did you?" Cole leaned over, his face so near Emily's that she could feel his breath. "I could even smell you, you were so close," he whispered.

Emily turned her head away from him.

Cole stood up and chuckled from deep in his chest. "Don't worry," he said. "I'll wait until your boyfriend gets here and let him watch us."

For a few moments, Cole paced the cabin. He stopped in front of one of a half dozen antique anchors Marty had mounted on the cabin's wall.

"Nice collection," Cole murmured.

Emily turned her head slowly so Cole wouldn't notice, and glanced at her watch. She wondered if there was any chance Marty might have found her offer of love so unexpected that he'd been alerted that something was amiss. More likely, she thought, Marty probably figured I've finally come to my senses. Emily looked at Tammy, huddled sullenly on the couch. Her bruises were turning from red to purple.

Thirty-five minutes later, Emily saw the headlights of Marty's Blazer coming slowly down the road toward the dock. Cole turned off the map light. He grabbed Tammy and jerked her to her feet and pulled her into the boat's narrow hallway, again holding the knife to her throat. Tammy seemed completely passive, but Emily saw a glint in her eye. She prayed that Tammy wouldn't do anything foolish and get them all killed.

"Get him in here fast," Cole whispered.

"Hey, beautiful," Marty said as he came across the deck and saw Emily standing in the cabin's door. He stopped before he reached her.

"I thought you were going to be wearing a teddy," he said. Suddenly, Emily saw suspicion register on his face.

"Come inside," she said, pulling on his arm. "Open the champagne."

He went with her. "Is everything all right?" he asked as he entered the cabin. He slid the door closed behind him, turned on the map light, and looked at Emily. As his gaze shifted and he looked past her shoulder, Emily saw his eyes widen in fear.

"Hello, Marty," Cole said. "I hear you've been expecting me."

"You put down that knife, Cole," Marty said. "You've got no problem with Tammy."

Cole came into the room and shoved Tammy onto the couch. He shut the knife, put it in his pocket, and pulled out the gun. "Sit down," he ordered Emily.

"This is no way to greet an old friend," Marty said. He smiled broadly at Cole. Cole pointed the gun at Marty.

"I want to go for a ride on your boat," he said. "Go untie the lines."

Cole followed Marty onto the deck, but stayed where he could watch the women as Marty loosened the ropes along the side of the boat.

"Start it up," Cole said to him when he came back. The big inboards rumbled as Marty turned the key. "Head toward Kimberling City. Go down the middle of the lake."

Marty put the boat in gear and pulled smoothly and silently away from the dock. Emily's heart sunk deeper into hopelessness as she watched the shoreline recede.

"Look, I don't know what you've got in mind here, but let's talk," Marty said.

"Talk about what?" Cole barked. "About how you're

going to make up for all those years you took away from me?''

"You can't hold me responsible for that," Marty said.

Cole picked up his empty beer bottle and threw it across the cabin where it shattered against the wall.

"You sent me up, Rose," Cole shouted. "All you had to do was tell the truth."

"We saw you stab her," Marty said.

"You saw her get away from me and take off running and fall over that bluff," Cole said. "I saw you two standing there in the bushes watching us. You knew I didn't kill Shirley."

Emily was stunned. What was she hearing?

"You raped her, and you knew she'd turn you in," Marty said.

"Raped her? I didn't even like the snooty bitch," Cole yelled. "She kept teasing me, and I was so drunk and she had me so turned on, I was just going to give her what she was asking for. These days they call it date rape. She wasn't even resisting me until she looked over my shoulder and saw you two. Probably figured you were waiting your turn."

"That's bullshit," Marty said. He glanced at Emily.

"That was when she started screaming like a maniac," Cole said. "I took out my knife so she'd shut up. I was going to let her go, but she grabbed at it and tried to turn it on me. I cut her a couple of times, but that wouldn't even have left a scar, let alone killed her. What'd they offer you to put me away?"

Marty ran his fingers through his hair. "She was Tom Mullen's daughter, man. He owned the whole town. Somebody was going to jail for killing her. That's the way it was."

"And it sure wasn't going to be you or Chick, was it?"

"We didn't do anything," Marty said. Cole came up

behind him and looked over his shoulder at the depth gauge.

"We didn't do anything," Cole mocked. "When I went to visit your old friend Chick last week, he claimed he didn't even remember what happened. He'd been lying to himself about it so long, he'd forgotten the truth. I killed him for forgetting."

Cole sat down on the couch opposite the two women. "But I know how it was, Rose. I figured out why you railroaded me. You and Chick decided you'd get yourselves off the hook with the judge and get rid of your competition at the same time. You knew I had the star-making song and the voice to sing it."

"It's not too late," Marty said. "I'll put you onstage tomorrow night."

Cole laughed. "Thanks very much, Mr. Marty Goddamn Rose," he said, "but I don't have any interest in joining your over-the-hill band."

Cole stood and walked to where the anchors hung. He yanked three of them down from the wall, crashing the heavy anchors onto the floor.

"Put the boat on low speed. I don't want you all piling up on each other." He reached into his pocket and took out the rose. He jerked the bloom from the stem and tucked it into Marty's shirt pocket. He patted Marty's chest and smiled. "Now get outside, and take the anchors with you."

Emily helped Tammy out onto the deck. It was a moonless night, but up the lake Emily could see the lights of the *Table Rock Showboat*, and she heard the rhythmic splash of the huge paddle wheels as it came into the main channel of the lake, headed in their direction. Marty carried the anchors out one at a time. Cole picked up a coil of rope from where it hung outside the cabin and tossed it at Marty's feet.

"Tie them up," he ordered. "Do her first," he pointed

to Tammy. "Around her waist." Cole opened the gate in the deck railing.

Emily watched Tammy glare at Marty as he knotted the rope around her wrists. "Now put it around her ankles and tie an anchor to her."

Marty didn't move. Cole put the gun against Emily's temple. "Do it," he yelled. When Marty had an anchor tied to Tammy's ankles, Cole popped his knife and cut the rope. "Now her," he ordered, throwing the rope at Emily's feet.

Marty came to Emily and tied her hands behind her back. She held her wrists a little apart, and Marty didn't pull the rope tight.

"I bet you've been wanting to do that for a long time," Cole snickered. "Now tie an anchor to her." He knelt down next to Tammy. He laid the knife on the deck and pulled at the knots around her ankles to be sure they were tight.

"Take us back to the house," Marty said. "I've got fifty thousand dollars in my wall safe. You can have it and walk away from all of this."

"I've already got your money," Cole said.

Marty stopped wrapping the rope around Emily's ankles.

"What are you talking about?" he asked.

"The fifty thousand dollars your agent sent my lawyer right after my song came out," Cole said. Emily could see in the darkness that he was smiling. "What's the matter? Didn't he tell you about it? I guess Zimrest figured he was going to make you a star, and it was worth fifty grand to shut me up. My lawyer put it in a bank account on Grand Cayman, after he took a generous cut for himself, of course. But after drawing interest for thirty years, there ought to be enough to get me by."

"Why'd you kill Zach if he'd paid you off?" Marty asked.

"I asked him one last time to tell the truth about my song. But he wasn't willing to do the right thing. I figured if he was the kind of man to turn me down, he'd be the kind to turn me in."

Cole stood up over Tammy. He looked at the *Showboat* as it came closer. He looked up at the sky. "Sure a lot of stars out tonight," he said. "I missed seeing the stars for thirty years. But a couple of days from now I'm going to start making up for lost time." He reached down and stroked Tammy's cheek with the gun barrel. "I'll be lying on the beach with a tasty little Caribbean whore."

Tammy used the only weapon she had. She bit down on Cole's wrist, right on the stitches, and hung on with the power and determination of a pit bull.

Cole screamed in pain and rage. The gun dropped to the deck. He ripped his hand away from Tammy, grabbed her, and slung her through the open gate, his stitches and flesh still in her mouth. Emily screamed. She watched the anchor tied to Tammy's ankles slide across the deck, catching by its hook on the railing. She heard Tammy hit the water. As water splashed over the side of the boat, hell broke loose on the deck.

Cole bent over to pick up the gun, and Marty lunged at him, knocking him to the deck. They rolled together in a frenzy, punching at each other and cursing. Emily worked frantically to free her hands from the ropes as she ran to the railing and looked over. Tammy was hanging upside down, struggling to free her feet, her head and torso underwater. Emily grabbed the switchblade Cole had left on the deck and sawed at the rope.

Behind her, Marty and Cole rolled toward Emily, and she jumped sideways to avoid being knocked down. Emily grabbed the life preserver hanging on the deck, slashed again at the rope until it separated, threw the knife into the lake, and jumped into the water holding the loose end of the rope tied to Tammy's ankles. Emily

knew if she let go of the rope, she would never find
Tammy in time under the black water. With one arm
hooked around the life preserver, she ducked underwater.
She couldn't see a thing, but she felt Tammy's weight
pulling at the end of the rope. She came up for a breath.
The houseboat was moving away from her in a slow circle, and the slap of the paddle wheels of the *Showboat*
was louder now. Emily pulled in the rope until she caught
a glimpse of Tammy's white blouse under the surface.
Emily grabbed hold of her and pulled her until Tammy's
head was out of the water. Tammy was limp and lifeless.

She kept Tammy's face above water while she clawed
at the cord around her wrists. She freed Tammy's arms,
and pulled her onto her chest on the life preserver, and
pounded Tammy's back. ''Breathe,'' she screamed at her.
''Breathe!'' Emily kept pounding. She looked over her
shoulder and saw the *Showboat* headed straight for them.

Tammy coughed up water and gasped for breath.
''Hang on,'' Emily shouted. The sound of the paddle
wheels was like a drumbeat. Emily kicked frantically
away from the path of the looming boat, paddling with
one hand and dragging the life preserver. Tammy opened
her eyes. She saw the hull of the huge ship towering
above them and screamed. ''Kick,'' Emily cried. The
boat was nearly on them. If they were sucked under,
they'd go straight into the paddlewheels and be crushed.
Emily kicked with all her strength. She heard the hiss of
the water along the sides of the ship's bow. Tammy was
paddling with one hand now, too, and kicking with her
bound ankles. The ship skimmed close behind them. The
slap of the forty-foot-tall paddle wheels was a deafening
roar. They were no more than eight feet from the ship.
Emily felt the water pulling them, and she kicked for her
life. Then the tug of the water lessened, and the ship
passed. Gasping for air, the two women lay still in the

water. The houseboat was circling back now in their direction.

Rocking on the life preserver in the paddle wheeler's wake, they saw Marty pull Cole to his feet and throw him backward. Cole's head shattered the glass door. He grabbed Cole again, stood him up, and landed a hard punch on his chin. Cole's head snapped back, and he dropped to his knees on the deck. His face was covered with blood. Marty kicked him in the stomach, and Cole fell forward, unconscious. Marty stepped into the cabin, turned the key, and shut off the boat.

In the water, Emily let out her breath and began paddling again with one hand toward the boat. Marty had the upper hand now. They were safe. Then she saw Marty come out of the cabin and pick up the coil of rope and an anchor.

"Marty," Emily called. They were only thirty feet from the boat now, but Marty didn't seem to hear her. He was wrapping the rope around and around Cole's limp body, weaving the anchor to him.

"Marty! Stop! Come get us," Emily shouted at him. He didn't look in her direction.

Cole, coughing and gagging on his own blood, was reviving. Clutching him by the rope around his neck, Marty slapped his face hard.

"Wake up, you dirtbag son of a bitch," he yelled. "You come here and think you can screw with Marty Rose." Marty slapped him again. "Your time's up, pal."

"Marty! What are you doing? Stop!" Emily screamed at him, paddling now with all her might toward the boat.

"He's going to kill him," Tammy gasped.

Cole's hollow eyes focused on Marty. He tried to move and looked at the ropes trussing him like a worm in a cocoon. He saw the anchor tied to his legs. Then his lips curled in a twisted smile, and with every bit of energy he could muster, he spit blood in Marty's face.

"I'll see you in hell, Marty Rose," he said.

Snarling with rage, Marty dragged Cole to the gate and heaved him into the murky depths of Table Rock Lake. The water splashed against the women's faces, and they saw Cole go down.

Marty reared back from the railing, then rushed forward again and looked into the water. There was nothing but a trail of bubbles. Marty watched the water until the bubbles disappeared. Then he straightened and looked at the women, frozen in horror.

"Thank God you're all right," he said. "Paddle over here, and I'll get you out." He squatted and held out his hand to pull them up. Emily could see it was covered with blood. She stared up at him, but it was impossible to see his face. The dim light from the cabin ringed his head like a halo.

"Come on," he urged. "Grab on."

"You have to call the police," Emily said, her voice quavering.

Marty's voice was as calm as the silent lake.

"What are you talking about?"

"You have to call the police," she repeated.

Marty stood up and looked down at the women in the water. "And just what exactly are we going to tell them, darlin'?"

Emily looked at Tammy. She was shivering violently. Marty stooped down again, and Emily took his outstretched hand. He pulled Emily onto the deck. Her legs were shaking, and she felt like she was going to throw up. She saw the gun lying at Marty's feet as he pulled Tammy out of the water. He straightened and kicked the gun, sending it sailing out into the lake.

Emily put her arms around Tammy. Marty looked at the two women and smiled at them.

"Too bad no one's ever going to know how Marty Rose saved your lives tonight."

✳ LAST SOUNDS ✳

Emily can hear the pulsating sound of the paddle wheels growing louder and louder. She tries to swim, but she can't move. The sound fills her head. She opens her eyes and sees Rocko lying beside her on her pillow, his purr loud as a buzz saw.

Anna comes through the doorway, carrying a tray that holds a steaming bowl of soup.

"Did he wake you up?" she says. "I've kept him out all day. I figured you and Tammy needed to sleep as long as you could, but he finally snuck in here."

She sets the tray on the nightstand, and sits down on the edge of the bed.

"Tammy's awake, too. She's in the living room. Do you want to come out there and eat your soup?"

Emily sits up. She feels disoriented. Her body aches.

"Is Tammy all right?" she asks.

"More or less," Anna says. She pats Emily's leg. "When you're ready, you can tell me what happened last night, if you want to. All I know was you sure wanted to come home."

Emily runs her fingers through her hair and feels the short tuft where Cole's knife had cut so close to her head.

She clears her throat. "I'm not sure what happened," she says.

Anna watches Emily, waiting to see if she's going to go on. After a moment, she stands up.

"Come on," she says, picking the tray up. "Before it gets cold."

In the living room, Tammy is on the couch, wrapped in an afghan. Her face is a mess, but she smiles at Emily as she sits down beside her on the couch.

"Your tea's almost ready," Anna says to Tammy.

On the television, a commercial ends and a shot of fireworks fills the screen. The announcer's voice comes on. "And now, live from the Crystal Rose Theatre in Branson, the Marty Rose Fourth of July Spectacular!"

There's Marty in his sparkling suit, smiling, bowing, waving at the audience. The camera pans to the crowd, three thousand people on their feet, shouting and applauding, eager for the show to begin.

Emily picks up the remote control and turns off the TV.